CASINO

Printed in the United States
by Piscataqua Press
32 Daniel St., Portsmouth NH 03801

ISBN: 9781798731222

CASINO

Royale

A Patrick Ingel Investigation

MURRAY SEGAL

TO BRIAN LIGHT

This book is dedicated to **Brian Light**, a longtime friend, who passed away on July 8, 2017. I first met Brian in early 2002 when I took my typewriter to his store, Hoyt's Office Supply in Portsmouth, NH. I thought he drove a hard bargain by agreeing to sell it for me for a 50% commission. Since there were no other stores around, I agreed to it. In about a week, the typewriter I had paid $20 for, sold for $400. Both of us made good money on the sale and I became a typewriter enthusiast. Brian taught me all about the techniques for buying, selling, cleaning and repairing the machines. What I didn't know about Brian when I first met him, was that he was the sole survivor of an experimental treatment for brain cancer. So, for the entire 15 years that I knew him, he was fighting this disease. Brian was strong, with a good sense of humor, and continued working for years. He was always congenial and never looked for sympathy. Something of a hellion growing up, Brian was loved everywhere he went, including the care facility where he lived his last years. He is missed by all who knew him, particularly his mom, Dottie, his brother, Tom, his son, Carter and me. Thank you, Brian, for making our world a better place.

TO JANICE WAYNE

I have seen many books dedicated to wives and other loved ones that one might think that this is a literary routine and almost meaningless. Trust me, this dedication has genuine meaning. There is no way in the world that this book, or any other of my six novels, would ever have seen the light of day without the help and reinforcement from my wife, Janice Wayne. She has encouraged my work from the very beginning of all my projects and lifted me up many times when I was ready to quit.

Writing and editing is hard work . . . trust me! Her editing skills and suggestions have been invaluable. In addition to her cheerful and unwavering support, she has also been my "I.T. go-to-person" who managed to solve the dilemmas of keeping the Toshiba working and dealing with the vagaries of Microsoft Word. Janice was always the last one to read each book for any last-minute fixes before they were sent to the publisher.

Thank you, Janice, from the very bottom of my heart. I love you dearly for all you have done for me over the years. My view of the future is brightened by your help and presence. We make a good team!

CHAPTER I

"BAM"

I duck instinctively and feel broken glass flying, mostly into the back seat. Quickly, I reach under the seat, grab my gun and let fly with a shot to the guy's left leg. I am a private detective, Patrick Ingel, by name, and have never shot anything at all, never. However, I practice shooting all the time at a range, under the supervision of an expert. So, I know how to shoot accurately. I drop him in his tracks and then jump out of my ancient pickup truck, kick his gun well out of reach and wrap his own necktie around the wound to stop the flow of blood. I am well aware that detectives take risks, but my practice is a quiet one. Never have I imagined a situation like this. Had I known where it would all lead to, I might well have let him bleed out.

As I am standing over the guy whose name is Tom Johnson, the focus of one of my few active cases, a young man runs out of the motel office and says to me, "I saw everything and have called the cops. If you need a witness, let me know."

"Thanks. I probably will need you. He fired first, and I had no choice but to drop him."

"Lucky you did. The guy is crazy."

As we are standing there, Johnson's nooner comes out of the motel room, runs over to Johnson, wailing at the top of her lungs.

In a few minutes, the cops arrive, along with an ambulance to cart him off to the hospital. This is the first time in my life that I have shot anything alive, not even an animal. I have a sinking feeling in the pit of my stomach as a police sergeant approaches.

"Sir, could you come over to my cruiser, so I can get a statement? You did shoot this man, correct?"

"Sure," I respond and take a card out of my pocket, hoping that as a private investigator it might cause him to treat me better than a "civilian."

"I just want to get an idea what went on here, before we take you down to the station for a formal written statement. Ok?"

"Sure, and don't bother reading me my rights. I am familiar with them. In a nutshell the guy you just hauled off to the hospital is named Thomas Johnson and he has been having an affair with the young woman your partner is interviewing in that cruiser over there. I have been retained by Johnson's wife, who will be filing for divorce. Johnson and his mistress came out of room number 7 over there, and he spotted me. He ran toward my car in a rage, drew a gun and got off one shot that shattered the rear window of my truck. I had no choice but to return fire and got him in the thigh. I got to him quickly and used the necktie to reduce the flow of blood.

"Is that his gun over there on the pavement, or yours?"

"That's his. Mine is on the front seat of my truck."

"Hold on and I'll get it." He gets my gun and puts it in an evidence bag and does the same with Johnson's.

"You have a license to carry?"

"It's in the glove box but I'm afraid it has expired."

"Oh, not good." He fetches the license from my truck and puts that in another evidence bag.

"Is that going to get me in serious trouble?"

"Well, the law's the law but it was lucky you had the gun since if the facts are as you say they are, the gun saved your life. I think the lieutenant and the DA will take that into consideration. I'll wager it will bring you nothing more than a slap on the wrist."

"A conviction on any criminal count would turn off some potential clients. If there is anything I can do to avoid that? I'd be beholden to you."

"Maybe we'll figure something out."

"Ok. Am I free to go after you take the written statement?"

"Yes."

It takes an hour for us to get to the station and take my formal statement. When we are finished, I enquire, "Are you finished with my truck?"

"Let me call the guys at the scene."

Five minutes later he informs me they are, indeed, finished with my truck. He drives me out to the scene. I drive the truck directly to a glass shop. An hour later the glass has been replaced. The cost of that will be added to the client's bill. She will get plenty of money out of him when they divorce, and I am in need of every penny that is rightfully mine. I am operating on a subsistence level here in New Haven.

I'm starved, so I head for the nearest Burger King and fill up with burgers and fries. I drown myself in coffee. Enough to enrich some Colombian coffee bean farmer and cover his expenses for about six months. Coffee plays havoc with my stomach. I drink it, nevertheless. That's good because the pain reminds me that nothing comes without a price in the free world. When I get back to the office, there is a calling card with a note on the floor just inside the door. I should point out there is enough space between the bottom of the door and the floor to slip a box of frosted flakes into the office. Small failings like this add to the charm of this dilapidated fleabag of a building.

The note simply says, "Please call me at your earliest possible convenience." The card has a Connecticut telephone number and the name "Roger Jones" on it.

This could be my lucky day. I have already wrapped up my cheating husband case and now it sounds like there was a new client nosing around. Concluding that Mr. Jones was a prospective client may have been a small leap of faith at this point, but I believe in the power of positive thinking. I pick up the phone and dial the number on the card. Luckily, I had just paid my grossly overdue telephone bill a few days prior.

"Hello, my name is Patrick Ingel. I am looking for Roger Jones."

"This is Roger Jones."

My goodness, Mr. Jones is in no better shape than I am. No secretary. Answers his own phone. Maybe I should just hang up right now. What the hell, give it a shot.

"Mister Jones, my name is Patrick Ingel and I just found your card in my office. What can I do for you?"

"I want to talk to you about an important matter, but not on the telephone. Can you see me after lunch? I am still in New Haven and would like to see you today."

Aha. I deduce from his comment that Jones does not live in New Haven and he has travelled here to see me. How's that for detecting? My hourly rate for him just went up 10%.

"Ok, I can move some appointments around. How about 5 o'clock?"

In point-of-fact, I have no appointments and virtually nothing to do except prepare a report for my angry client. That could wait until the photographs of her cheating husband were ready. I was not equipped to print them out and needed to sponge off a frequent client of mine who happened to be an attorney. Who better to sponge from than a slimy lawyer?

"That will be fine. Confidentiality is extremely important in this matter. Please don't talk to anyone about this."

"You have my word on that." Besides, I think to myself I don't even know what "this" is.

"Good. See you at five."

This begins to sound like something big. I celebrate the occasion with an early dinner at Louis's. I hope there is a big enough fee in this job to get my dinner money back. Little did I know. Rather than speculate what this guy might want with me, I sit at my cheesy desk and think about the past. I met my ex-wife, Penelope, in high school and we fell in love at first sight. She was even more beautiful then. Being 17, I didn't so much care about the smart and talented part of her. Of course, both of us vowed our love to be a forever thing. Forever lasted just fifteen years. At that point, we called it quits. Rather, Pene (her nick-name) called it quits. I suppose money was the problem. We never had much of it and Pene was spending most of her time taking care of the house and the kids. I was too dense to notice her discomfort with our situation. My excuse was simply that I spent all my time working my ass off at subsistence level jobs. Still doing that, but my guts are telling me that is about to change. Little did I know.

After the divorce Pene struck it rich, marrying a successful stock broker who provided all the goodies she wanted: big house, clothes, college tuition for the kids and everything else that went along with a high-income lifestyle. Weekend trips to the "Big Apple" to take in shows and to shop, the installation of a swimming pool at their large and rambling house that looks like a desecration of a Frank Lloyd Wright design. Several months off in the summer for a trip to Paris. Weren't people buying stocks in the summer? Good. Maybe his brokerage is drying up and that was one last fling. I wallowed around in this sea of self-pity for several hours. The end of my trip into this sea of self-pity comes with a knock on the door. Oh my god, it's 5 o'clock already. I run my fingers through my hair (honest, I did), went to the door and opened it.

There stands a distinguished looking man dressed in what

I take to be a hand tailored suit that could have come from New York or even London. He is wiry and about six-foot. He is dark skinned and has a chiseled look about him. Face all angles. A knowing tough look on his face. I stop gawking after about fifteen minutes and take his extended hand.

"You must be Roger Jones. Come on in." Sharp detective, yes?

"Yes. And you are Patrick Ingel. You look just like your pictures."

My pictures? What pictures? He must have spent some time checking me out if he has pictures.

"I am. Have a seat. Please excuse the mess here. Been out working and haven't had a chance to straighten up." I have the distinct impression that he doesn't buy any of that bullshit. I need acting lessons to improve my ability to snow people.

"Well, good that you are so busy. I came to see you about a possible job. Do you think you will be able to take on a large and important project in the immediate future?"

See that, he didn't buy any of my dream about being busy.

"Well, why don't we talk about it? What is the work about? I may be able to take it on sometime soon."

Yeah. But not until tomorrow morning, I think to myself.

"I prefer that you answer my question, first. I cannot talk to you about the project until I have a firm commitment from you. It is a very important project to us, and I don't want anyone to know that we have hired you. I know this may be a strange request. I can just about guarantee you will want the project and that it will be very profitable for both of us."

"OK. I'll take it on as long as I don't have to kill too many people and I will certainly honor your request for confidentiality if I decide not to take on your project. Shoot." Who, I wonder is *we*?

Hey, I thought that was funny as hell, but he doesn't crack a smile.

"I represent the Casino Royale, located in Voluntown, Connecticut. I understand that you were born in Norwich, so I'm guessing you are familiar with the area. By the way, I hear that you were involved in a serious ruckus this morning."

He obviously has done a complete background check of me, right up until this very morning. I resolve right then to play it totally straight with him.

"Roger, I am familiar with the area. But I have never been in your casino or any other one for that matter."

"That's ok. You will have full access to all the information you need, either directly or indirectly through me. So, let's get down to the basics of the problem as we know it now. Put simply, the Casino has developed leaks. As near as I can tell they started about a month ago and have continued unabated to this day, despite our best efforts to find out what is going on. We have tons of experience with security, so I am truly embarrassed to admit we have no idea how the money is getting out."

"Have you hired anybody else outside the Casino to help you? My resources are frankly quite limited."

"No, indeed. You are the first attempt to get some insight into the problem. Time is important here. It is the highest priority for us to plug these leaks. The losses are large and increasing every day. You will have our backing and cooperation in every way."

"Hold on just a minute, Roger. I think I am a good detective but as you can see, my business is not flourishing, and my financial assets are as low as they could be. I mean to say survival level. I am teetering on the edge of closing this office. Perhaps you should consider a larger firm with more personnel and assets." Don't you dare, I think to myself.

"Thank you for being so open about your financial condition, but we already know that. We want to keep exposure of the problem to a minimum. That means as few people as possible working on it; someone who is way out of the public eye and doesn't live anywhere near the Casino and is not known there. You fit that profile perfectly. And you should have no worry about assets because we will provide all the money up front that you tell us you need. If we hired a large firm to investigate that would mean more people and the greater the risk that the word would get out. You understand money could not be disappearing from the Casino without the involvement of someone on our staff. Probably more than one and perhaps a large group."

"But they will know that you have an investigation going on, even if it's only you who are doing it. Right?"

"They may very well be ignorant of the fact we know of the losses. You see they are very clever and I believe what they are doing is reducing the likelihood we will find out about the leak. I believe what they are doing is manipulating the revenue numbers to hide the shortages. The very last thing they want is to put management on notice of the outflow. I don't want them to know that I even suspect what is going on. If they knew that I know there is a leak they would no doubt shut down for a while and then start up again when the heat is off."

"I think we have a deal Roger. It sounds like an intriguing problem and I am looking forward to working with you."

"Excellent. How familiar are you with casinos?"

"Well, as I said, I have never been inside one and I know nothing about what goes on in one nor how they work. Except what I have seen in the movies."

"That's good. Your face will not be familiar to any of our employees, which is what I want. I'd like you to take a trip over to Casino Royale and simply walk around and get familiar with its layout, where the various games are, where the biggest crowds are, and so forth. No investigating. Just look around and get comfortable as you can with the place. Make a few small bets. Pay attention to **all** of the facilities at the Casino both inside and outside. You also need to rent a small office in the general area, maybe Norwich, perhaps New London. But not in one of the smaller towns where you might stand out."

"How will you handle the expense money?"

"I'm not sure yet but probably with cash because I want to minimize the opportunity of a paper trail between us. I will let you know in a day or two. In the meantime, you might want to clean up whatever work you have remaining here. We are buying your undivided attention and want nothing to distract you from this job. Shut down this office and put an ON-VACATION sign on the door. You should have your mail forwarded to the new office. When I get back to you with the initial expense money, we will sit down and talk about a preliminary plan for the job. These leaks are mounting up; losses we can't afford. Speed is important to us, as you can understand."

I am recalling an article I read recently on the financial problems all the casinos are dealing with. I make a mental note to check this out soon.

"Ok then. It's good to have you aboard and I will be back here sometime tomorrow afternoon. That should give you time to wrap things up."

"It will. See you tomorrow."

I sit there for a few minutes, savoring the present and anticipating the future. The present be dammed. All I see in the future are good things. Some money. Maybe enough to replace my 15-year-old pick-up truck. An enhanced reputation because I swear to myself that I will crack this case. Maybe even a vacation in some warm locale like Bimini, Key West or

San Diego. I don't remember the last time I felt so good about myself. But first order of business. Call the kids. I dial my ex-wife Sheila's number and get a busy signal. God, they have four different land lines. How could they all be busy at the same time? I guess I am just not used to telephones being busy. I call back fifteen minutes later and finally get Sheila to answer. I get a bit nervous at the sound of her melodious voice.

"Sheila Brown. Who's calling please?"

"Hi Sheila. It's me Patrick."

"Oh you. What do **you** want?" Her voice has immediately taken on a hardened tone.

"I just want to speak to the kids."

"Do you think you might just stop by and see them someday?"

I notice a bit of sarcasm and maybe some venom in her voice. It's not hard to notice.

"Don't give me a hard time. I'm going on a business trip and need to talk to them before I leave tomorrow afternoon. Please put them on the phone."

"Business trip? I see nothing has changed. Is some disgruntled creditor chasing you out of the city? Hold on a minute. I'll get them but don't talk too long. Marjorie is getting dinner ready for them and it will be ready in 15 minutes."

Her way of reminding me they have tons of money. Margorie indeed. Enough dough to hire a full-time baby sitter, nanny, cook. Cynthia, who is 10, gets on the phone first and we spend a few minutes getting up to date. Finally, I can feel her interest fading so I tell her why I called.

"Sweetheart. I am going away for a time on a big new job, so I won't be able to talk to you in a while."

"Ok, Dad. Here's Mark."

She is through with me just like that. I can hear the disdain in her voice. Just like her mother.

"Hi Dad, how are you doin'? Cynthia says you are going away on a new job. What's it all about and how long will you be away?"

"Markie, this is a very big and secret project and I pledged not to talk to anyone about it. I don't know how long I will be away, but I will call you as soon as I get back. And come to see you."

"Hey, we have a vacation coming up soon. Do you need an assistant?"

"Thanks for the offer son, but this is a one-man job. Maybe in a couple of years I'll put you on the staff. I'll see you soon. I love you."

"Bye dad. I love you too."

I decide to treat myself to a steak and French fries at Louis's restaurant that evening. A detective must keep up his strength. Besides, if I haven't already told you, I like to eat. After dinner, I crank up my Toshiba and start a search. I find two articles in the New York times from 2012 and 2016 about the difficulties casinos are having. I find that these two casinos, Foxwoods and Mohegan Sun, are among the largest in the world. A fact I was not aware of because I had never been to any casino in my life. They have suffered very large drops in revenue. As much as a 40 percent hit. Wow. Most businesses would not be able to survive a drop of that much. What keeps the casinos going is their locations on Indian tribal land which means that they are insulated from normal bankruptcy requirements. A mess of new casinos, some of which are in New England, are providing more competition. Gambling casinos are springing up all over the country. At Foxwoods and Mohegan Sun every adult member of the two tribes has been getting a $100,000 a year stipend just for being alive. I wouldn't be surprised if some of the dead citizens were also receiving the stipend. Every year since the casinos first opened, year in and year out. By the time the article was written, this freebie had drained 500 million dollars from the casino's revenue and had been recently stopped. Now I begin to understand why Jones was so eager to plug all leaks he could find. His poor little Casino Royale is not even mentioned in the article.

I hand crafted a lovely cardboard sign the next morning. It said simply "On Vacation." A small lie. Detectives must lie sometimes. I also put my cellphone number on it and left a message on my land line that would inform any callers that I was on an extended vacation. I arranged for the Post Office to hold my mail until I could give them a forwarding address. I am contemplating running to the apartment for clothes and stuff when there is a knock on the door.

"Hi Mr. Jones. Come on in."

"I will. Time to call me Roger. I noticed your sign on the door. Is that your current cellphone number?"

"Yes, it is."

"Well you better take it off. I have a new throw away cell for you that only I will know the number of. This is just another precaution for anyone trying to trace your whereabouts. Have it on always, so I can call you day or night when it is convenient for me."

"Ok."

"Now. Before you leave town, I have arranged for you stop at J. Press Men's Store, so they can measure you and pick out some good clothes for you to wear while you are at work. When they are done, they will mail them to you at a small house that I have rented for you in Norwich. I also have set up a checking account. I will see that the balance never goes below $10,000. I will check from time to time to see if you need any more money for the work. Now, when you get settled into the house, I want you to visit The Casino Royale in Voluntown. Make sure you get into all the public areas inside the buildings and outside on the grounds. Take some money with you and do some light gambling. Make small bets so you are not conspicuous and stop if you start winning more than a small amount. Just stop and cash in your chips. Stay away from the slot machines because there is the unlikely chance you might win one of the giant jackpots and your photo would be all over the place. Look at what the customers are wearing and try to match their dress. Another way to try and meld into the crowd. Get as familiar as you can with the movements of the staff but do that quietly. Don't forget it's almost certain some of them are involved with the loss of money. I expect it will take a substantial amount of time to really cover the place thoroughly. I am not expecting you to waltz in there and solve the problem overnight. Make sure you see the Casino operating during all times of the day and night. They NEVER close."

"Really?"

"That's correct. The tribe never expected that to happen, but it did from the very first day. The doors have never been closed. Now, make sure that none of our employees suspect you are a private detective. Should anyone ask and there is no reason they should, we are in the process of inserting your name into an existing small stock brokerage firm in New London. We've also fixed you up with a new identity. Nice to meet you Arnold Kowalski. We have a driver's license in that name and a social security card. They are forgeries, since any attempt to obtain the real thing would carry with it the risk of exposure. I have full confidence in you, and I know you will do a good job. There is a bonus for you at the end of the project, in addition to your hourly rate, for every hour you work. The amount of the bonus will depend on how successful you are in plugging the leak. The minimum will be $100,000 and the max could be 7 figures depending how long it takes."

I stop myself from gasping at the size of those numbers.

"I am perfectly comfortable getting my hourly fee," I say. "A bonus is not necessary."

"Suspected you would say that but it's not your decision to make. Go get started. Good luck and be careful, my friend. I have no idea who these crooks are, so watch your back. If you have any idea that you are being followed, call me immediately."

"One last question. Can you give me any idea what the scope of your losses are?"

"Sure thing. We don't know the exact amount of the theft because of their manipulation of the books. Our best guess is about 10 million dollars a year or even more. That would be at least $20,000 every day."

"Sounds more like a flood than a leak. Ok then, I am on my way."

I am reminded of the great Molasses Flood of 1918 that devastated the north end of Boston when a gigantic tank full of hot molasses burst and swept through the neighborhood along Commercial Street at 35 miles per hour, killing 21 people.

Leaving my old office, I go straight to J. Press where they measure me for a couple of suits and god knows what else. They already have my forwarding address in Norwich. I pick up my rental car at National. After they deliver my truck back to my apartment I lock the doors and leave it parked in the driveway. The rental contract and payment arrangements are already taken care of by Jones. A brand-new Cadillac Escalade. Driving it is like floating on a cloud. As different a feeling from my rattling pick-up truck as day is to night. I could get used to this. I suppose I better because it will probably look strange driving around with my mouth open and a dazed look on my face. Oh, Penelope! If you could only see me now. I thought about stopping by her house, just so she could get a look at this car, but I quickly came to my senses and go into the apartment to pack some clothes and other stuff. An hour later I am zipping along Interstate 91, northbound, trying to keep the Escalade at the speed limit. It is like trying hold an Arabian racehorse to a slow walk. Then again, I have never seen an Arabian racehorse let alone ridden one. Maybe when this job is over, I'll buy myself a stable full of race horses. I exit 91 to Route 66 (not that Route 66 but Connecticut 66) at Meriden and drive to Middletown, home of Wesleyan University and the widest main street in the universe. Then over the bridge to Portland and on toward East Hampton, where I grew up. Well, almost all the way up. Still growing. Stay tuned. Nostalgia brought me on this route. Too bad I can't stop and visit with some old friends like the lovely Lee Burnham, a high school classmate of mine, and her husband Richard.

I am reminded of my promise to Jones about staying inconspicuous, so I drive right on through without stopping. Memories come flooding back of living in what was once the Belltown of America, famous for producing millions and millions of bells of all kinds. Toys, as well. They are all gone now, although the owner of the last factory to survive, Bevin Brothers, was promising to rebuild his plant after a disastrous fire last year. Matt Bevin, coincidently the Governor of Kentucky, is the owner of the plant site which was now just a pile of rubble. The town population is about 15,000 people compared to the 1,500 or so back then. Ten times as big but no one worked here anymore. Just a suburban bedroom community for Hartford and other nearby cities. My heart clenched up a bit as I skirted the shore of Lake Pocotopaug, a once very active recreational center with many large vacation hotels along its shore. Including one owned by the family of my old friend Ann Amenta. Mostly all gone. Remind me to tell you about the legend of Princess Pocotopaug sometime, but not now. On to Norwich. I take Route 2 from Marlboro directly into Norwich. No more time for sightseeing. Time to go to work. The address of the house rented by Roger is 5 Cuprak Road. This turns out to be just off the end of Route 2. The single-family ranch style house is in a residential area filled with similar homes. It was only about a mile from the Bacchus Hospital where I was born. Norwich is a small city of about 40,000 souls. At least that was what Wikipedia told me when I had unpacked all my earthly belongings and had turned on the Toshiba.

My family moved from Norwich when I was a year old. I confess I have minimum memories from that time. This is bad, especially for a detective. Anyhow, Norwich's population jumped about 15% in the twelve years from 2000 to 2012. I expect much of this population growth is due to the cities' proximity to the casinos. Maybe all of it since I was not aware of an increase in any other job producing industries in the area. Even with the reduction in revenues, the casinos employ close to 20,000 people. I decide to do some preliminary scouting of Casino Royale from the outside, today. Just to get to get a feel for the layout of the buildings and other facilities. But first I drag out the Toshiba and get some aerial photos of the place. To my untrained eye, it looks gigantic and contains many buildings, hotels, restaurants, night clubs, and a parking garage. And of course, the casino gambling areas. There were many acres of undeveloped land earmarked for future expansion. I wonder if that would ever happen, given the proliferation of casinos all over the country. It has access via Route 138 in Voluntown. It looks so massive that I decide to forget about any looks at Mohegan Sun for at least another day and maybe more. Even without seeing it in real life, I begin to relate the size of the place with its revenue information and the size of its debts. I dress in casual clothes and get the Escalade onto Route 138 for the short trip to the Casino in

Voluntown. I take the only road into the site and park in the circular garage at its center. The garage is connected to two hotels on either side of it. The patrons do not have to go outside to get from the garage to either hotel. And they could quickly satisfy their need to gamble since the covered, all season walkways, are lined with slots. I walk directly into the Casino from the garage and begin to look around. The place reeks of money and yet, many of the patrons milling around and playing the games are rather slovenly dressed. I know there are areas reserved for high rollers but not here on the ground level. It is covered with row after row of slot machines that are ringing and dinging, along with an occasional shriek from a jackpot winner. I was not used to such hustle and bustle, but I try to be nonchalant and just drift with the flow. I don't have any idea how many machines there are, but they are all being used. I see 25 cent machines, 1-dollar ones, and 5-dollar ones. I assume there might be others of higher denominations, but I don't see any here on the ground floor.

Back to the two hotels for a look around. There are direct connections to both hotels, one to the north of the garage and one to the south. The one at the north is a Hilton Inn. The lobby, check in level of the hotel, is quiet and elegantly furnished. I conclude that its guests are mostly higher income folks. Incoming guests are nicely dressed, most with shirts and ties under tailored suits or sport jackets. I make a note to check in sometime during my investigation. I suspect there are some ultra-expensive suites on the top levels. I intend to leave no stone unturned. Back through the garage to the southerly hotel I find a Days Inn. Nicely done but not nearly as elegant as the Hilton. No doubt fewer high rollers stay here. I will manage to spend a night here as well as the Hilton.

I casually walk back through the Casino at the ground level to the parking areas in the rear. There are three large lots which I judge could park hundreds of vehicles each. There are security personnel patrolling the lots in jeeps, so I stay only long enough to scan them. The northerly most one is reserved for employees, the middle one for patrons and the southerly one is full of buses. I notice one of the security guys is watching me, so I hold out my hands, palms up to suggest that I might have lost my car. Wrong move. He drove over and got out of the Jeep.

"Sir, can I help you with anything?"

"No thanks. My wife is a bit drunk in the Casino and I thought I would locate where she parked our car before she is too drunk to remember. I see it over there in the middle lot."

"If you need any help getting her out to the car let us know and I can call someone to assist you."

"Thanks, but we haven't been here very long. I will cut off her drinking and steer her to the slots. Might cost me in the long run but that's what we came for. Yes?"

"Have a good time, but don't take too much of our money home with you."

"Thanks."

Whew. I congratulate myself as I walk back into the Casino, for being so quick with a believable story (read lie) to take the heat off. I learn a lesson in those few minutes. If the parking lot security guys are that sharp, then I'd better be prepared for the inside work, since that's where the money lives. I also learn that I am pretty good at making up stories (read lying) on short notice.

Enough detecting for the first day, so I make my way back to my car and take off, back to Norwich and Cuprak Road. After a refreshing shower, and dressed in some of my new duds, I take out my Toshiba to search for a suitable restaurant. All that walking at the Royale had drained my energy. I find just the right place, Prime 82, located on West Town Street just off Route 395. Not far from my new temporary home on Cuprak. The head waiter shows me to a quiet table and takes my order for booze. I decide on a bottle of Jermann Chardonnay from Italy for only forty-seven dollars. I don't know if I will be required to file an expense account with Jones, but I got the impression from him that a few dollars on food and drink would be no problem. This was a far cry from Louis's place in New Haven. I can get used to this high living, but it probably would take me about ten minutes to get the hang of it. Practice, practice, practice. I relax and have a delightful meal. Can't go home and put this $125 dinner to bed, so why not go back to the Casino and look around some more in the early evening? I drive straight there.

Wanting to look inconspicuous in my new duds, I go to the top floor where the high enders live. I saunter around the gaming tables making a few bets here and there. I am on a winning run, so I leave the tables after a few minutes because I couldn't seem to lose. The crowd up here at the top was well dressed, so I don't think I stood out in my dark suit. I take turns at roulette, blackjack, and even a few hands of poker. In just forty-five minutes I had won $150.00 taking just about every hand that I played. I walk around for a while longer and then make my way to a cashier to convert my winnings into dollars. There are six windows open at this location and all six are seeing a lot of buying and selling of chips. At the back of the cashiers' position, I can briefly see several large bags, which I assume contain cash on the way to the bank. I can't get a good look because I am next up at the line I am in, and anyway, they were at the very back of the room, too far away to see any details.

"Good evening sir. Are you cashing out now?"

The cashier is a tall thin man who reminds me of my client, Roger Jones.

"Yes, I am, Tom. " He has a name plate on his shirt that tells me who he is. In fact, all the floor workers and security people have name plates. I feel sure there are other security people circulating on the floor without any name tags. I guess there are security cameras in the ceiling as well. I make a mental note to check this out with Jones, the next time I see him. Lots to learn about the place.

"Thank you for your patronage. I hope I will see you again sir."

"You're welcome." On this floor I have become a "sir."

I know he hoped to see more of my Ben Franklins, but did he really want to see me? He hadn't known me for long but maybe he detected something warm and charming in my demeanor. Nah, it was all about Franklin. I make another mental note to ask Jones for a list of all the security personnel, all the cashiers and other employees handling the cash, and everyone in the accounting section. I suppose this will be a rather long list, but I expect I will need it sooner or later. By this time, it is close to midnight, so I call it a night. Before I go to bed, I make a list of groceries that I need to buy. I made enough cash at the Casino to pay for dinner and groceries for a week or more. Even though I am on an expense account, one gets tired of restaurant food after a while. My culinary talents are limited but I do know how to scramble eggs and cook bacon. Ain't I a multi-talented dude? I make a mental note to learn how to cook some basic meals and set the alarm for 5am. That should get me to the Casino by seven.

I don't know if this happens to anybody else, but I almost always wake up about 30 minutes before the alarm goes off. So, here I am taking a shower at five the next morning. After scrambled eggs and bacon, (see I have learned to cook already). Off to the Casino and I'm parking the car in the central garage at 6. Amazing. The garage is not full, but I estimate there are 300 cars already parked. Inside, on the bottom slots level, there seems to be as much activity as yesterday afternoon. There are no windows in most of the gambling areas, so I suppose if you are feeding an addiction, there is no "outside", no "day", "no night", no nothing, except the lure of the gambling devices in front of you. It feels like drug addiction to me, but I have never had that pleasure either so what do I know?

I hear the same sounds from the slots and from the occasional winner as I walk the floor. And then suddenly something new. As I pass by a row of slots, I see two older women wrestling at the end of the row of machines. They continue to whale away at each other until they both fall to the floor, still locked in combat. Two female security persons quickly separate them. Apparently, a peace treaty is negotiated. The women, who both looked to be in their sixties, return to the machines and resume feeding them with quarters WITH BOTH HANDS as fast as the slot will take them. I wonder if they are spending social security money.

Walking up to one of the security guys who had been watching the two scuffle I ask, "What was that all about?"

"Well, nothing to worry about. Happens all the time. Some of the patrons play certain machines so much, that when someone else comes along and starts to play on it, a territorial battle ensues."

"I see. Your job must require a lot of tact and negotiating skill."

"Well, it does. I've worked here for four years and I have seen many of these battles. The Casino has an excellent training program. We are encouraged to be as gentle as we can. Obviously, we want to keep everyone happy. Are you a reporter?"

"No just a visitor in town for business. Well, keep up the

good work." Sure, keep everyone happy so they will keep coming back with their Social Security money. Come to think of it, I am on the receiving end of this cash flow myself.

My education continues. Saddest thing I've seen in years. I wonder how many of these folks are really spending Social Security Checks, rent money and even food money. You would think they would get the message that the deck is stacked against them and in the long run, the Casino is the only consistent winner. I make it a point to put these thoughts away. After all, I am working for the Casino, and if they didn't win, I was out of a job. I make my way up to floor number two and find a poker game where I think that skill would give the players a chance. I sit at a table with five other players and introduce myself only as Bill. I play for about an hour and increase my $500 stake all the way up to $520. Well I could make $20 an hour working in a carwash. I take my $20 and leave the table. Two hundred dollars goes at the roulette table and another $100 at blackjack. The dealer's faces are all pleasant and they smile frequently. But one can't read anything else into them. Part of their job training must be to learn how to show no emotion and they certainly do not. A high-speed elevator whisks me to the top floor (the 6th) in seconds. This floor is for the high rollers and it shows. The customers are better dressed, quieter and fewer in number. Ah, but they have the same disease as those customers on the lower levels. You can tell by the intensity with which they play. They, no doubt could afford their losses better, but said losses are certainly much larger. I leave after 15 minutes, through the outer lobby to the elevator. Just a few slot machines here and they were of the 5-dollar variety. It feels as though the down elevator is much slower than the up one. Maybe they wanted to whisk the customers into the place with their money and then made it more difficult to leave. Probably my over active imagination at work. In any event I am through for the day. Hunting for a cocktail lounge on the way home, I settle on a nice-looking place named the G Bar in downtown Norwich. I worked hard today and feel a need for a cocktail or two. The Toshiba tells me to have a steak and at least one cocktail at the "G Bar," downtown on Thames Street, named after the Thames River. Or was it the other way around and the river was named after the street? Another detecting job as soon as I could get someone to pay for it. Anyhow, I made my way to this classy establishment in my new duds and in my new SUV.

"Good evening Sir. Would you like a table in the dining room or in the lounge?"

"Let's try the lounge, thank you."

"No, thank *you*. Your server will be Gineen."

After a short wait, a gorgeous blonde waitress (Hey, I'm old fashioned) wiggles up to my table.

"Can I get you a cocktail or a glass of wine, sir?"

"I'm not sir. My name is Arnold." I come perilously close to giving her my real name. Maybe I should stand in front of the mirror for a few hours and introduce myself to Arnold. A slip like that at the wrong time could get me in bad trouble.

"I'll start with a martini or two and then go from there. Extra dry please."

"Certainly Arnold. Would you like to eat here in the lounge or in the dining room?"

"It's very comfortable here, so here I will stay."

Besides, I doubt very much if there are any waitress in the dining room as lovely as you, I think to myself. Even before my second martini, I am conjuring up images of Gineen lying naked on my bed on Cuprak Road. Well, I mean in the house on Cuprak Road. Yum. Just looking at her working her way around the lounge causes a bit of a stirring below the belt. A man needs love as well as food and it has been a long dry spell.

You might even call it a drought. After my third martini, I am busily engaged in scheming just how I might get Miss Gineen into my clutches. I could use my subtle approach and just ask her to bed. Or I could be more direct and ask her when will we have sex? Turns out I don't need any of my clumsy dialogue for as she brings me the fourth martini, she stops to talk.

"I don't remember ever seeing you in here before. Is this the first time? As handsome as you are, I know I would remember."

"Indeed. As beautiful as you are, I most certainly would remember you. This mutual admiration society can be over right now. I have just recently moved here from New Haven. Now that the subtleties are behind us, when do you leave this place and where shall we go. Your place?"

"Not possible, I have a roommate. Where are you staying in town?"

"I have rented a house on Cuprak Road, not very far from here."

"Good. Your place it is."

Hard for me to believe this beautiful creature has just invited me to bed. Maybe it's the Martinis. Or maybe she just needs someone to talk to. I hope not.

"I'm glad we have settled that. When do you get off work?"

"I'm on the early shift today so I'm done in fifteen minutes."

"One problem. I'm not fit to drive. Particularly with such a precious cargo."

"Not a problem, I will drive"

"But how will we get back here after we both have had drinks?"

"We will figure that out in the morning when you wake me up. Judging by that bulge, you are ready to leave right now."

"Hey. No fair, you've been peeking."

"Can't blame a nice girl like me. I'm particular about who I sleep with, so I haven't gotten laid in some long time."

"I'm honored. I only hope I live up to your expectations."

"Leave that to me. You will"

With those words and a look that seemed to pierce my chest and go right to my heart, she leaves me to take some orders from other customers. My kind of a woman. You could say a woman after my own heart. No mysteries with her, so I don't expect to have to waste any time figuring her out. A relief for a detective who lives on mysteries. She is so direct, I start to wonder if she might be a pro.

It's a long fifteen minutes until she quits work and waltzes over to my table. Nah, pros don't work slinging hash in a restaurant.

"Let's get out of here sweetheart."

"Ok. Let's go."

She leads me out the door to her car which is a small, but nice-looking Mercedes. Maybe a few years old.

"You sure my SUV will be ok overnight here on the lot?"

"I'm sure, but if it will make you feel any better I will move it over to the other side of the lot under one of lights. They stay on all night."

"That would be better. Thanks."

"No thanks necessary, it's part of the service."

I give her the key and she quickly parks the SUV on the far side of the lot. She comes back and gets into the driver's seat but, instead of starting the car, she slides over, puts her arms around my neck and plants her full, soft lips on mine and slips her left hand down between my legs. I am starting to get nervous. This girl is really acting like a pro. I can't be that charming. Or can I? It has been a long time.

"Oh, my, I don't know what to say."

"Well sweet, how about you just say your address and let's get out of here?"

I spit it out. She puts the car into gear and roars off. It's quiet in the car during the short ride to the house. Just inside the door, she throws her arms around my neck and kisses me quite thoroughly. Wow, my kind of a woman, or did I already say that?

When we got inside the door I ask her if she'd like a drink. "Would you like a drink?"

"What I want does not come in a bottle. Where is the bedroom?"

We fairly race into the guest bedroom and start shedding our clothes without bothering to close the door. She has black stockings with matching underwear. Her lush body doesn't need the assistance of the sexy attire. I am immediately aroused and so is she. She pushes me back on the edge of the bed and in a matter of just a few minutes we both have orgasms together.

When I catch my breath, I feebly whisper, "Oh, my God, you do that one more time and I'm done."

"Shut up and lay back on the bed."

No question who is in charge here and never have I enjoyed taking orders from a woman more than at this moment.

"Whew, I'm exhausted. I could sleep for a week." I utter these words in a hoarse whisper.

"Not on your life, sonny. The party has just begun. You've got five minutes to rest and that might be all that you get the rest of the night."

Now, the orders have gone too far, and I start a minor rebellion. Or at least I thought it was minor.

"That's a bit more than I bargained for. I have work to do starting at 5am tomorrow morning, so I must beg off for the rest of the night.

"You're kidding, right?"

"No. I am serious. As much as I'd like to spend the rest of the night making love to you, it just isn't possible."

"I should have known this was too good to be true," she growls as she jumps off the bed and heads for the shower.

"Give me a break, Gineen. I really have some very important work to do."

"Oh yeah. What's that?""

"All I can tell you is that it is important to my career and means a lot of bucks to me. My client would kill me if I disclosed anything about the job."

"Right. I've heard stories like that before. You're just like all the rest. If all I mean to you is a one-night stand, and not a whole night at that, I'm out of here just as soon as I can wash all traces of you off in the shower. It was a mistake to even have come here with you."

WHAM. I think the bathroom door might rip off its hinges, she slams it so hard. I guess I should have told her about my need to get out early before we started fooling around. Ten minutes later she comes out of the shower and starts to make her way to the front door.

"Come on Gineen. I really like you. You are the best thing that has happened to me in years. I want to see you again and get to know you. Give me a chance. Please."

"Sure, just tell me exactly who or what's so important that you must abandon me."

"Gineen. I just can't tell you right now and probably won't be able to until the job is done and that might take weeks or months. I am pledged to secrecy. Give me a break. I like you. I want to see you again."

"You've had your chance. I hope I never see you again."

"Hey, at least drive me back to my car."

"Not on your life, you SOB."

And out she goes, slamming that door as well. Here I stand with another botched romance staring me in the face. I need lessons on how to treat a lover but where do I go for that? I call a cab for a ride to my car and then return to the house for some sleep before I have to get on the job in just a few hours. I make it to the Casino Royale by five.

I immediately get the largest cup of coffee I can find and began my early morning tour. Jones was right, there was a surprisingly large crowd on the ground level and the slots were ringing away as though it were 11 am. I walk out to the rear parking lots and notice fewer busses but the other two lots were nearly full. I play a few games on each level and even sit down for a round of bingo. Lord the crowd here is almost as large as the slot level. During the four hours I'm there, my thoughts keep drifting back to Gineen. I wondered if she really meant it when she said she never wanted to see me again. I genuinely hope we can get together again. Probably too soon to stop by the G Bar and try to worm my way back into her good graces. I'm also bothered by the fact that I have no clear picture of how I'm was going to solve this case. I need to talk to Jones. I hope he calls soon. We need to get together and try to work out an approach. Plan some of the details. Should I call him on the throw away cell that he gave me? No, I decide, I will wait for him to call me.

CHAPTER II

Well, a guy can get dumped by a woman he thinks he cares about but that doesn't mean he stops eating. Nevertheless, that evening I avoid the G Bar and drive to a restaurant named the Prime 82 for dinner. A good choice. None of the waitresses or patrons show any interest in me. One glass of wine is my limit. Not to suggest that I was interested in another liaison. Not on your life. Maybe I could have done a better job of explaining my need to keep quiet about the job. But how? I hoped I'd get that chance soon. I'd build a plan to get back in her good graces no matter what it takes. Flowers? Candy? Wine? Dinner at the best restaurant in the state? Maybe even take her to the Royale for dinner, entertainment and a bit of gambling. Now there's a plan worth exploring. Nothing in my contract that prohibited me from bringing a date to the Casino, just so I don't let her know that the "secret" project is there. I like it.

Now I must sell it. First some flowers sent to her at her workplace since I don't know where she lives. Skip the wine since she has plenty of that where she works. Then a carefully crafted invitation for dinner at the elegant Blue Danube Restaurant on the top floor of the Royale. Hellava plan, don't you think? How could she resist? To be on the safe side I need to run this by Roger the very next time he calls. I drive home at 11:15 and set my alarm for 10 the next morning. I spend the night watching The New England Patriots and Tom Brady beat the Pittsburg Steelers at Gillette Stadium. Another trip for Brady and Coach Belichick to the Super Bowl. Atlanta beat the

Packers easily in the early game, so they advance to the Super Bowl as the NFL champs. No call from Roger, so I go to sleep without any sort of an idea just how I was going to start to solve the main problem. The next day. I decide to get a look at the competition to the Royale, namely Foxwoods and The Mohegan Sun, located in nearby Ledyard, Connecticut just across the Thames River from our family burying ground. Appropriate. My dad was a bit of a gambler. One of his genes that I missed.

The New York Times had published an article last year which detailed the problems both casinos were having due to the increased competition from other casinos. Casino Royale was not the only competition, but it was the closest. I thought it probably was the most competition for the other two. Would they find a way to make money again? Who knows? Anyhow, I make the short drive to Ledyard and spend four hours at each casino. Both are huge compared to the Royale with all kinds of features we didn't have. They both seemed very busy, but I just couldn't get it through my head how they would survive much longer. I suppose if you were a debtor you had nothing to lose and everything to gain by letting the casinos try to struggle out of their financial mess. Still, I wonder about current expenses. The workers' salaries had to be paid and outside vendors weren't likely to provide services on credit. It seems to me that if those expenses aren't brought into line to cover operating costs, the casinos could ultimately fail, American Indian ownership notwithstanding. Not to be mean, but any such failures would benefit my client whose Casino Royale was already making money and spending within their means. I wasn't privy to the information but I'm guessing their debt, if they had any, was under control. It was likely the "leak" was their major problem. I am bound and determined to take that off their list of concerns. From my lips to God's ear. I spend four hours at each casino and then return home, hoping to hear from Roger soon.

It's quiet and lonely at the house and compared to last night, very dull. I really miss Gineen. Too soon to call her, but I reckoned not too soon to send flowers. I call a local florist and order a dozen roses to be sent to her club. I decide to go "soft" with the card and have it inscribed with the message, "With warm feelings from a Secret Admirer." I nearly jump out of my skin when my cell rings and for a moment I can't remember where it is. I get it on the fifth ring and sure enough it's Roger.

"Good evening," says Roger. "I thought I might stop by our place tonight for a bite to eat. Ok with you? We can have some pizza and some beer. Is that convenient with you? I'd like to talk about approaches to begin working on."

"Yes, it certainly is. Do you have a preference what you want on your pizza?"

"I do prefer pepperoni and extra tomato sauce. Sam Adams beer would be my choice, but I am flexible when it comes to beer. Is an hour from now convenient?"

"It is, I will see you then."

I hang up the phone, careful not to mention his name. I'm not a detective for nothing. And I don't watch movies for just their entertainment value. I find a pizza joint not far away (in fact I find about 20 of them within an easy drive) and order a pizza to be picked up in 30 minutes and then drive to a liquor store where I buy a case of Sam Adams. You don't want to be caught short when it comes to beer. Back home, pizza in the oven to keep it hot and beer in the fridge to keep it cold. Right on schedule Roger shows up.

"Come on in, Roger. Good to see you. I was hoping you would call, and you did. We must be wired."

"Good to see you too. Let's eat first and then go over my agenda."

"Ok. Come on into the dining room. Did you watch the Patriots slam Pittsburgh?"

"Oh, indeed I did. We had the game playing on our giant TV's at the Casino. I'm not sure that was such a good idea because gambling activity slowed down during the game. I hope it recovered in the aftermath, but I haven't seen the final numbers yet. In any event, it was a predominantly happy crowd."

We continue the small talk for another 15 minutes while we munch on the pizza and sip on the beer. I clean up the bottles and the residue of the pizza and take it to the kitchen.

"Arnold, let's begin with a summary of your activities to date."

"Okay. I've spent a few days getting familiar with the Royale facilities both inside and outside. As of this point, I think I have a basic understanding of the layout of all the floors in the Casino but not the two hotels. I will get to them next, but I don't think much goes on there that we need to worry about."

"I don't agree with that. Until we have solved this problem, we need to look at everything. So, follow through with our plan and spend a couple of nights at each place."

"Okay. I will. This would be a good time to bring up a subject that was not our original agenda. The last few days I have struck up a relationship with a local woman who works here in Norwich at a restaurant and bar. Would it be ok if I took her out with me to the Casino? It would look normal for an out of town businessman to show up now and then with a good-looking woman."

"Just so she doesn't know what you are doing here. I don't see how it could hurt and it might very well help. Tell me about her."

"Well, I don't know all that much about her yet, her name is Gineen and she is a waitress at the G Bar here in town."

"Before you start getting serious about her, let me get a profile on her."

"Sure. Good idea." (I hope).

"I'd like to hear what inroads you have made becoming familiar both with the facilities, the staff and the gambling activities."

"As I indicated, I have spent several days casually studying the physical layout of the building. I have spent time on each level of the Casino itself, identifying the various games played in all the areas. I have tried a few of them making small bets and wandering from game to game, not letting any winnings get large and mostly losing. I have spent very little time on the Penthouse level, so I don't know very much about it.

"As far as the personnel go, I have talked briefly to only one of the cashiers on the third floor whose name is Tom. I also had a small chat with a security attendant in the parking lot who noticed me walking around. He thought I might have lost my car in the large outdoor lot. Outside of those two I have not spoken to any of the employees except a few nameless ones while playing the games. I followed your advice and did not play the slots, but I did spend time there. Finally, I spent four hours at Foxwoods and four more at Mohegan Sun. I researched the financial troubles the two were having. Amazing how they have managed to survive."

"True, but we hope they will continue to survive not just to maintain good inter-tribal relations, but I believe there is a synergistic relationship between the three of us and Royale would suffer if the other two disappeared. Thankfully I don't think that will happen, at least anytime soon.

"On another matter, have you given any thought to how much and what kind of additional resources you would need to dig into and below the operational aspects of the Casino?"

"No, I really have not had time to think seriously about that, save to decide that I clearly will never crack this case from the outside all by myself. I will need help, no question. How much and what kind, I don't know yet."

"I think you are making good progress and I am going to deposit another $5,000 in your checking account. Suppose I call you next week?"

"That's good. It will give me time to do some more looking around and more importantly some more thinking."

Roger sticks out his hand and I grab it. He turns and lets himself out, leaving me the job of cleaning up the dishes and remnants of the pizza. Ah, the privileges of rank. His presence in the house had disguised my lonely feeling. I am really missing Gineen and really, I hardly know her. Something is going on with me. I had no desire to go out or to seek other companionship. Am I getting old beyond my 39 years or could I be really falling in love? Maybe I've started to understand that I am never going to reunite with my ex-wife, Pene. Gineen had shoved all thoughts of her out of my mind. I suppose if nothing good ever happens between us, I still could thank Gineen for that. Shit, was I growing up at this late date? What a revolting thought. None of my friends would recognize me. What friends? Damn, I don't have any. All this introspection has worn me out. To bed. I can't get to sleep due to the images of Gineen floating through my brain. Tomorrow, I must talk to her. I spend another hour reading on my kindle and finally conk off about two in the morning.

I do a round of exercises and eat breakfast at 9 am and decide that I have to get Gineen out of my mind. The only way to do that is to see her and hope that we can be back together again. I hire a messenger and give him a note to be delivered to her when she begins work this afternoon. In it I simply beg her to see me and that I plan to stop by sometime today.

I have all day to return to the Casino Royale problem and I

do a lot of thinking about it, particularly Roger's request to know what additional help I might need. I make a paper list, jotting down all the assets I can think of.

1) A list of all the employees by name and where they worked. Include both inside the Casino and outside in the parking garage and lots. Include both hotels. Given that there will be natural turnover, update the list every day.

2) A more detailed list of all the employees who handle cash, except for those on the gambling tables. Include their employment history from their initial date of employment to the present and any criminal involvement even for minor infractions such as parking violations. Update this weekly.

3) A daily compilation of total revenue for the entire Casino by hour for every day starting one week prior to my employment. Update each day.

4) A detailed list of each employee in the accounting and auditing departments by shift. Update each day.

This would be a large work load and would require several employees who could compile the lists quietly without anyone knowing what they are doing. Hopefully Roger has a small number of people he can trust implicitly. He could plant them in the proper office and their work could begin very soon. If he couldn't trust anyone on the staff, then outsiders would have to be found, cleared, and trained. That would slow the job considerably. By the time I finish ruminating about the future of the project, it is late in the afternoon. I opt to go to the G Bar and see if I can get Gineen to come out to dinner. When I get there, she looks at me from across the room. Even at a distance I can tell the look is cool. That's better than cold. She sends one of the other servers to come to my table and makes no move to come over and say hello.

"Hi. Gineen asked me to take your order."

"Ok. I'll have a dry martini. And could you please ask Gineen if she could please come over for a minute. Tell her I won't keep her but a minute or two."

"I will."

She comes over a few minutes later with my drink.

"Thank you for the flowers. They are beautiful. Here's your martini. Can I get you anything else?"

"Gineen, I want desperately to talk to you and I was hoping you would come to dinner with me. No strings attached. If you still want me to disappear from your life, I will do it."

"Alright, but understand, this is not a date and I haven't got much to offer you except for a few hours of talking."

"That's fine. I understand completely. I am going to call The Blue Danube restaurant on the penthouse level of the Casino Royale to see if they have room for us."

"Arnold, the Burger King just down the street is good enough for me."

"I know it would be, but I really want a quiet place where we can talk and think. Humor me."

"Well ok. Tell me how to get there and I will meet you in about an hour. How should I dress?"

"Well it's an elegant place, but you could wear a burlap bag and still be the most beautiful woman there. I'll see you there, soon."

"Thanks for the endorsement, but I'm all out of burlap so a

simple little black thing must do."

"If you're sure that you won't ride with me, I'll give you directions on how to get there. It's not far nor hard to find."

"Thanks, but I will drive myself. See you there."

I think I detect a softer tone to her voice, but maybe I am just imagining it. We meet in the lobby of the Royale an hour or so later. A speedy elevator whisks us to the penthouse level in a matter of a few seconds. The Maître De' seats us in a table in the far corner of the restaurant, away from most of the other diners. I had everything pre-arranged with Roger's help. The waiter drops a wine list off and leaves to go back to his station at the door.

"Vincent will be your waitperson and he will be right over."

Vincent turns out to be a stately 50-year old gentleman, garbed in a black-tie tuxedo.

"May I get you something to drink?" He sets down two cute little bottles of ice-cold Poland Spring as he speaks.

"I'll stick with the water for now, but I may have some wine with my meal," answers Gineen.

"The same for me."

There's a rather cold silence when Vincent leaves the scene. I say nothing, while I pick up the menu and begin to study it.

"Just why did you invite me out, Arnold?"

"You know why, Gineen. I've missed you terribly. I had hoped and still do, that you would give us a chance. I'm falling in love with you. You must know that. If you don't feel anything for me just say the word, and I will disappear from your life for good. It scares me to say that. I've had nightmares that you would tell me to leave. I think you must have known most of that. Why did you agree to have dinner with me tonight?"

"If you must know, it's got nothing to do with dinner. You absolutely must know that I have feelings for you. Amidst the chaos of the other night certainly that must have come through. I just ended up feeling that you had tossed me on the scrap pile over a thing as small as some work."

Just then I spot Roger heading our way. I stand to grab his outstretched hand.

"Hi, good evening, Roger. Meet Gineen Walker."

"Nice to meet you Ms. Walker. Arnold has told me much about you, but you are far more beautiful than he told me."

"Roger, if you are trying to get me in trouble, you are off to a good start. You must have something better to do."

"Well. I can see that you are not in a sharing mood tonight. Hard as it is to leave, I think I have your message. You two have a great evening and if there is anything you need let me know. Gineen, you are in good hands with Arnold and you are both in good hands with Vincent. Oh, by the way Arnold, that profile I told you about turned up positive. Take care."

"See you later, Roger."

As he leaves, Gineen turns to me with a quizzical look and asks, "Who is that guy?"

"Gineen, he is the general manager of the Casino. He runs the place from top to bottom."

"I think I'm getting it. You are working for him. Aren't you?"

"Gineen, I am about to break a pledge of silence about my work..."

"No, no, no I don't want you to do that. Please let's just finish our dinner and then we'll talk some more. But I can tell you right now that I do not want you to break any promises to anyone, because if you can break a promise to someone else you can also break one to me. Let's order."

"Ok, but I can tell you right now that you are already more important to me than any job, good as it might be." I motioned to Vincent and he was hovering over us a few seconds later.

"Yes ma'am. What can I get you?"

"I'll have scallops and a glass of champagne."

"Certainly, and you sir?"

"I'll have a sirloin steak. And you might as well bring a bottle of champagne."

When he leaves, I reach across the table and take her hands. Looking me in the eye, she says, "Arnold please take it slow. I am still very fragile."

"Sure." I could see some tears forming in her beautiful blue eyes. "This time we do it your way. Your happiness is my only concern. Even at this early point in our relationship, I know that I would never do anything to hurt you."

"Thank you."

Our meals arrive 20 minutes later. We both pick over our food with little enthusiasm.

"Arnold, let's get out of here. Take me home."

We go hand in hand to the elevator and down to the first floor. As we are making our way across it to the garage, she suddenly turns toward me and puts her arms around my neck and buries her head in my chest. I feel her quiver and hold her tighter.

"Arnold, I can't promise you anything, but I know I want you to take me home and stay with me. And hold me."

"I will, and you needn't promise anything until you are sure about your feelings."

With that, we go to her car and I drive her home after getting directions from her. Her place is a rather new condominium. It's a roomy place on the first floor, nicely furnished with a woman's touch.

Once inside, she leads me directly to the bedroom and holds me close.

"Arnold, I need a lot of holding. We can go from there when we see what develops. I can't promise anything. I just feel so fragile. I need to feel your body against me. I feel cold. I will be back in a couple of minutes. Get naked and under the covers."

With that, she shuts the bathroom door. I take off my clothes, as directed, and slide under her down comforter. When she comes back into the bedroom, she slides under the covers and puts her arms around me. I hold her tightly. I can feel her body quivering as though she were crying. Moments later the tears start to flow as she pushes her face into my chest.

"It's ok, Gineen. I'm here and will be here all night. Relax and try to sleep."

"I need you to love me. I want to love you back, but I don't trust either one of us."

"Just take some deep breaths and close your eyes and let your body go limp."

She does take some deep breaths and I feel her body relax a little. There is no way that voluptuous body would ever go limp. I try to think about anything else besides my urge to make love to her. It's obvious that she is in no condition for sex. Before too long her breathing slows down, the tears stop, and she finally drops off to sleep. I think how different it is with her. It's not solely about sex. I am starting to love her deeply and want nothing to get in the way of that. I will never again be content with a one-night stand. I fall off to sleep myself, and dream all night long.

My built-in alarm wakes me at seven the next morning. I quietly sneak into the bathroom without waking her but when I came out, her lovely red hair is spread across the pillow and her green eyes are just opening. This is a picture that I hope I will see each morning for a very long time.

"Good morning, love. Can I get you a cup of coffee?"

"Nonsense. What you can do is get into this bed and make sweet wonderful love to me."

"An offer as you can plainly see that I am in no condition to refuse."

As I slip under the covers she wraps her arms around me and whispers in my ear, "Love me, Arnold."

"Are you sure you are ready for this?"

"Buddy, did you hear what I said? Love me thoroughly and completely and leave no stone unturned."

"Your wish is..." her lips smother any further conversation.

It is everything I hope it would be, except not long enough. Not a problem, there is an encore coming. I can feel it coming. She brews some coffee. We sip it slowly. Neither one of us says a word. After a few minutes, I am lost inside her again but this one is slow, and we make tender love to each other. We drift off to sleep and don't wake up until late in the morning.

"Did you dream?" I ask.

"Yes, did I ever. Arnold, for the first time in ages, I dreamed about making a baby."

"Oh yeah. With who? Robert Redford?"

"With you, dummy."

"That's sweet, but neither one of us is ready for that."

She forcefully punches me in the gut. "Why not, we've known each other for at least two days? And see that it doesn't happen until I say the word."

"You got it. Now do your wifely duties and make us some breakfast."

"Sexist. Making you breakfast is not what I was put on this earth for. Don't push your luck."

Later, as I'm wolfing down my bacon and eggs, I look at this beautiful woman across the kitchen table and say, "I need to tell you what I am doing at the Casino."

"No, you don't. I don't need to know."

"Maybe not, but I need to tell. I have decided I don't want to have any secrets from you. Not now. Not ever. It's a very simple story. There is a leak at the Casino. Someone or some group is stealing money. My job is to find out how it's disappearing and stop it as soon as possible."

"I sort of guessed that you were working for the Casino. Are the losses large?"

"Absolutely. No one knows exactly how large they are but certainly in the millions. We think they are manipulating the revenue numbers to disguise the fact that revenue is decreasing. They are smart as hell. It won't be easy to catch them. I have only just started. If I solve the problem I have been promised a very large bonus."

"This sounds like it could be dangerous, with all that money involved."

"It might be, and I would understand if you would like to distance yourself from me for a while. I was recently involved in a shooting that had nothing to do with this new job for Roger. And it's probably my imagination, but I keep feeling that I am seeing a couple of faces all too frequently."

"Not on your life. I am a member of the stand by your man club. You must have put a lot of money into this job. What exactly did this shooting involve?"

"I was snapping some photographs of a cheating husband. He spotted me and came after me with a gun. Fortunately, he missed. But not by much, and I had no other option but to drop him with a shot to his leg."

"Wow. You do live a dangerous life. That guy will, no doubt, be looking for you. Yes?"

"Well, said guy is going away for a few years. But he does have two brothers who may come after me. Since that affair, I find myself constantly looking over my shoulder. So, again, it would be prudent to separate from me."

"Not on your life. Don't you understand that I am starting to love you?"

"Sure. But that doesn't mean you can't put some distance between us. If you ever got hurt because of something I did, I doubt I could handle it."

"Well Mr. Kowalski, get used to having me close. Have you lived here for a long time?"

"Ok. Best offer I've had all day. And no, I have been here for only a few days. As for the question, I lived with my ex-wife in New Haven. For years."

"Children?"

"Yes. Two. A son and a daughter. My ex-wife Penelope has custody of them, but I see them often. She struck it rich. Her husband is a stockbroker with a flourishing business. She has everything she wants. I got nothing from the divorce, but our debts. Now you know most everything about me. You are hooked up with a middle aged, poor and struggling private detective looking for a big break."

"Who is very good looking, smart, and kind!"

"And your life story?"

"I am twenty-nine years old and I too, am relatively poor. I do, however own this condo where you are currently shacked up. I was born and brought up in western Massachusetts. A middle-class town and a middle-class family. My father and mother never seemed to get along. When I was 18, they split. My father left town and I haven't seen him since. I felt like I would be a burden on my mother, so I struck out on my own, gradually working my way down here. I have supported myself mostly by working as a waitress and bartender. I suppose you could say that my good looks have paid off very well. Single men in nice bars and restaurants tend to tip well. I've had a few flings here and there but none of them have been very long lasting nor satisfying."

"I am beginning to find out that your physical beauty is not the best part of you. It's the inner beauty and all that stuff."

"Arnold, I've been snowed by experts almost my whole life, so knock it off."

"No really. Before I met you, I became very proficient in snow jobs. You have changed all that. My one desire is to finish this job and take you out of this place, preferably someplace warm, and have a family. A normal life. I'll do whatever it takes to get there, even give up detecting."

We talk for another hour about all the things we want to happen to us in the future. The time flies by. Before I know it, she has her arms around my neck and is whispering in my ear, "Do you have time for a nooner?"

"Gineen, I am a very busy man with lots of work staring me in the..."

I don't get the rest of the sentence out of my mouth due to a luscious set of lips pressing on mine.

She backs off and looks at me with a questioning tilt to her eyes.

"Since you put it that way let's see if we can find the bedroom."

"Don't have time for that. Just push your chair back and let me sit on your lap. We'll see how that works."

It works extremely well.

CHAPTER III

It works so well that the lunch hour flies by. Why wouldn't it with a menu like that? Before we can think about food, my throw-away cell rings.

"Hello," I answer.

"Hello Arnold, this is Roger. It's time we sat down to begin to put together a plan for solving our problem. I assume you've had lunch by now (he should only know, best lunch I've had in ages). I'd like to stop by in about fifteen minutes."

"Roger, I'm not at the house just now. I am with Gineen at her place. How about an hour and a half?"

"That will do. Say hello to your lovely woman for me."

"I will. See you at two thirty."

"Well, judging what I heard of your side of the conversation, that must have been Roger."

"It was. He says hello to you."

"Really?"

"Yes, really. In his business, you learn to ID quality in people or you don't survive. He is not always right about that, witness the current problem he has. He is right about you, Gineen. I suppose you heard that I am going to see him at two thirty. That gives us enough time to have lunch of the food variety."

"Sure, let me clean up and put together some sandwiches and brew some coffee."

"Great."

After splashing some cold water on my face and scarfing down a roast beef sandwich, I drive over to the house. Roger and I both arrive at the same time and go into the house to scheme.

"Roger, before we begin, I must confess to you that I had to tell Gineen a little bit of what I was doing here. We've gotten very close and I felt she needed to know for her sake and for mine."

"I wish you hadn't done that without asking me first, but now that it's a done deal we will make the best of it. If this happens again, it will be the last time."

He is seriously pissed at me. "It won't happen again, guarantee it. By the way, I've been thinking that Gineen might be some help on the project. She is very popular at her bar and restaurant. Men tend to loosen up around her and she might just be able to stumble on some leads."

"Now that she knows what you are doing, she could be useful. But before you get into any more details with her, talk to me about it."

I tell myself not to go this way again, unless it's a matter of life or death.

"Ok. Now let me go over some of the information I hope might be useful in breaking this case. They are mostly lists. You tell me what is possible and what isn't. First, I'd like to see a list of all the employees on the complex and where exactly they work. Given normal turnover, this should be updated periodically."

"That won't be a problem. It's something that is already available. As manager of the complex, I will have no trouble getting you a copy and updating it. What else?"

"Ok. Second, a detailed list of all those employees who handle the money once it gets into the cashier locations. In other words, exclude those employees working the tables. I'd like to see their initial employment application and a record of any criminal activity, even down to parking tickets if we can get at that information."

"Their initial applications are easy for me to get. Parking tickets are another matter and we should both give some thought to how we might obtain that information, if you think it is really necessary."

"Ok, I will. It's just a matter of checking how truthful they are, even down to the smallest criminal activity. Next on my list, Roger, is a daily compilation of total revenue for the entire Casino complex, including that of the two hotels and the parking facilities. I'd like to see such a list for each day for a week prior to my employment."

"Arnold, that is also easy for me to obtain for every operation except for the hotels. It's possible I could get the information if the hotels have this data, but I don't know enough about their operation to be sure. I will talk to them and find out. Let you know. What else?"

"A list for each employee in the accounting and auditing departments showing the shifts they work each day. Again, begin this the week before my employment and up to the present with daily updates thereafter."

"It's obvious that you have been giving the problem some serious thoughts, Arnold, but that is what you were hired for. How are you fixed for money?"

"I've spent very little of your money so far. One question. If I needed a couple of trustworthy people to help with some of the work, would you make them available and would you be comfortable having them work with me?"

"Arnold, I think I have two senior employees who could work with you. But again, let me think about that and get back to you. I will call you as soon as I have the data you asked for. I guess that will take about two days. Let's meet back here on Thursday. Say about 1 pm."

"Good, see you then."

Most of the rest of the afternoon I spend at the house thinking about ways to solve this problem. Is there a way to do this without using any other personnel, either insiders or outsiders? I don't see how, but maybe I'll get a brainstorm before Thursday's meeting. One technique to check the money flow I've read about is the marking of bills with ink invisible to the naked eye that shows up under ultraviolet light. Maybe using bills with consecutive numbers. Both techniques would require looking at the bills before they are deposited. That sounded like a lot of work. It could be done by people who do not know who the bills belong to. On the other hand, this would require knowing which cashier the bills were going to and would mean a switch as the bills are delivered to the cashier under study. It seems clear to me that the stealing was going on after the bills reached the cashier's station. How could the switch be made without raising an alert? Something to discuss with Roger. The money is not counted until it gets into the cashier's station, so maybe Roger himself could seed a batch or two with either inked bills or bills with known serial numbers. Damn. That would mean the bills had to be examined before they got to the bank. How to do that? There might be a way, but it would probably involve another switch. This kind of tracking seems much too much work. I doubt it is practical.

It's 4 o'clock before I know it. Time to shut down my brain before there is a serious short circuit.

Gineen will be at work in a short while, so dinner with her will have to be at the end of her shift. Rather late for me but maybe I can last. I decide to try a drink or two at some other place and then get together with her when she leaves work. I consult the Toshiba brain since mine was in doubtful condition. It directed me to the Harp and Dragon Pub in downtown Norwich. See, the Toshiba is so smart, recognizing that I am Irish and ordering me to an Irish Pub. Maybe if I ask it would lead me to the perpetrators at the Casino. I get to the pub in a very few minutes and decide to sit at a table instead of the bar. A waiter takes my drink order and plops a menu down as he leaves to fetch the martini. Oh my, corned beef and cabbage is on the menu. This changes everything. I couldn't turn down one of my favorite meals. Gineen will have to eat without me. Corned beef and cabbage beats love every time. No, wait. I could bring her over here after her shift. Love AND corned beef. A winner!

I notice the customers at the bar are particularly rowdy even for an Irish pub. Most of the noise seems to be coming from one gent who appears to be buying drinks for the entire crowd. There is something vaguely familiar about him. From my table, I can only see a partial profile of his face. I wonder if he could be one of the philandering husbands from a case of mine in New Haven. I take a trip to the men's room, so I can get a better look at his face. Nope. Not from New Haven, but maybe I've seen him at the Casino. Lord, this could be a breakthrough, but I can't be sure. After a successful trip to the john, I go back to the table, being careful not to expose my face to him. He seems to be well on his way to a falling down drunk condition, so it probably wouldn't matter if he saw me, but better to be on the safe side. My detective instincts are kicking in. I have another martini, being careful to pace myself.

In another 30 minutes my unknown friend is indeed falling-down drunk, and his buddies have to help him off the floor. I see the bartender call a cab for him. When it arrives, they haul him outside and presumably throw him into it. My waiter returns looking for another drink order, but I let him know that I have to drive. When he returns with my bill, I speak to him in quiet tones.

"That guy who just fell off his chair at the bar created quite a ruckus."

"Yes, I'm sorry if he disturbed you. He comes here often and buys drinks for everyone at the bar."

"Well, he certainly seems like a generous man."

"He is. Works at the Casino and sometimes, like tonight, he overdoes it."

I really wanted the guy's name, but I decide not to push my luck with the waiter. There should be an easy way to get his name without appearing to be snooping. Ah, I'll come back with Gineen for dinner and put her to work. I pay my bill and drive over to the G Bar.

"Arnold, I didn't expect to see you for another couple of hours. Can I get you a martini?"

"No thanks, I've already had a couple and we have some work to do when you finish here. I'll tell you about it later. I don't suppose that you could get off early, could you?"

"It's a slow weekday night and the other girls can easily cover for me. I will tell them right now."

She goes to the bar and briefly confers with the bartender and the other waitpersons and then returns.

"Let's get my coat and get out of here."

When we get to the car, she gives me a big hug and asks, "What's the job we need to do? Will it wait until you've made love to me?"

"Unless you want to do it here in the car. It must wait a while. I'm taking you out to the Harp and Dragon Irish pub for corned beef and cabbage."

"You made me quit early for corned beef and cabbage?"

"No, no. There's a little bit more to it than that. I stopped there before, on my way here, and happened to see a guy there who was buying drinks for everyone and ended up falling-down drunk."

"Not very unusual for an Irishman, Patrick. You should know."

"Hey, watch your tongue. Don't you dare insult my fellow Irishmen. We have entered a new era in my life which is all love. So, have a heart. Anyhow, I thought I recognized this chap. The waiter told me that he works at the Casino. He visits the bar regularly. I didn't want to push my luck any further, but maybe, just maybe, I have stumbled onto my first serious clue about the Casino thefts. I need to put a name to the face and that's where you come in, Mata Hari. You are going to get his name from the bartender right now. If you are successful you not only get the satisfaction of helping to solve this crime, but you also get a corned beef and cabbage dinner, half my fee, and love all night long until I collapse."

"Money and corned beef don't interest me much, but the all-night loving does. You better not go back on your promise or I'll spread the word that you are a wimp. Let's go. The quicker I get his name the quicker I get to ravish you. I am starting to feel that I can't live without you. It's a good feeling. One that I've never come close to having before."

After getting a table at the Harp and Dragon and ordering the corned beef and cabbage, I ask Gineen how she was going to get the guy's name.

"Piece of cake, lover. I go up the bartender, tell him I heard there was a gent in here before who worked for the Casino and ask what his name is. Very easy and simple. Even you could have done it."

"Maybe, but I am trying to stay in the background. So, go ahead."

Gineen saunters up to the bar talks to the bartender briefly and the returns to the table.

"Nothing to it. He says everyone here knows him. His name is Samuel Lightfoot. I said he was not my friend and thanks."

"Good job. Here comes your corned beef and cabbage so chow down. You will need lots of energy for tonight's performance."

"Oh, ok. Maybe we could do it right here on the table. What do you think?"

"They might not let us back in again."

"Arnold, now that you have a name to go with the face, what's your next step?"

"I'll see what Roger might have in mind when I see him on Thursday. That will give me a whole day to do some of my own scheming."

"How come you just don't call him right now and move the meeting up a day?"

"He doesn't want me to call him unless it's a life-threatening emergency, so I'll honor that instruction."

"That's ok with me detective, cuz it gives us tonight and most of the day tomorrow to be together. Finish your damn corned beef and let's get home. You know, I never considered the condo to be my home before. It was just a house. But now it does begin to feel like a home when you are in it."

"I'm going to take the rest of this meal home with us, so you can make corned beef hash for tomorrow's breakfast like a good wife."

"Treat me right tonight and you will get a boatload of hash."

I pay the check and we walk arm and arm out the door to the parking lot. Outside I draw her close and kiss her beautiful lips.

"That was a nice surprise. Let's get home."

I awake next morning to the noise of pots and pans coming from the kitchen and a delicious aroma of something cooking that drifts into the bedroom. I would have thrown my robe over my jammies for the trip into the kitchen. Only I didn't have a robe. Oh yeah, no jammies either.

"Now there's a vision of middle aged manliness coming into my kitchen. No. you are not allowed to eat in the raw because it would distract me so go shower and dress. Shirt and tie required but you can forget about a jacket."

CHAPTER IV

Breakfast was great. Corned beef hash never tasted so good.

"Well missy, do you have anything in mind for today?"

"It just so happens I do. While you were showering, I took the liberty of consulting my computer and found a grand place in Voluntown where we can get some fresh air, sunshine and a bit of hiking. And don't call me missy"

"Hiking? Have you gone daffy? It's too cold for that even if I wanted to and had the right clothes to wear."

"Stop your whining and do the dishes while I locate a store where we can get you some dungarees and hiking boots."

"Lord you are beginning to sound like a wife. I spent a pile of Roger's money for nice clothes and you want me to wear dungarees and boots?"

"You haven't heard anything yet. Aha, here's just what we need and at a store not far away. Let's go."

"Hey, I haven't finished the dishes yet. You go and pick out whatever you think I might like."

"No way, I don't know you well enough for that yet. Someday, if all goes well. Leave the dishes and we will do them when we come back."

We drive the few miles to the store and buy chinos, jeans and hiking boots with some more of Roger's money.

Back home, I put on the new clothes, while Gineen does the dishes.

"So where are you taking me to try out these duds?"

"A place in Voluntown called Mount Misery."

"You are nuts. I'm not ready for mountain climbing. Let's just walk around the neighborhood for a while."

"Do you want everyone to know what a wimp you are? It's just a small hill which will not tax you at all. Barely seven tenths of a mile long with only a few steep rocky grades. Follow me."

Gineen drives us over to the trail in Voluntown, not far from the Casino. Hell, it didn't look too rough from the bottom. I follow her for a few hundred feet to a point where the slope starts to steepen dramatically. I start to get breathless.

"Ok, time to stop for a little rest and some water."

"It's not time for resting, we have barely gotten started and I don't have any water. We won't need it. Come on or I'll push you off the edge. I should have brought a length of rope, so I could lead you along like a donkey."

"I resent being called a jackass. That's it. Damn, I'll race you to the top."

"No racing. Just start walking. Keep pace with me. After all I'm just a mere slip of a woman, Mr. He-Man."

Gineen makes it to the top in about 45 minutes and I follow a few minutes behind her. My legs feel wobbly and my lungs are begging for air. When I get to her, she's sitting calmly at the edge of the rocky trail, admiring the view.

"Look at that view. Wasn't the climb worth it?"

"I suppose it is," I gasp. "Now call for a helicopter to take us back to the car."

"Funny."

"Well, at least show me to the elevator."

"Even funnier. Come on. By this time next year, we won't be able to tell you from an Olympic athlete. Have to enter you in the Boston Marathon. You're a detective. You can't always be shooting people. Someday you may actually have to fight one of the bad guys with your naked hands."

I decide to clam up right there before she has me fighting the world's heavy weight champ in Las Vegas. We get back to her condo just in time for her to go to work. I avoid telling her that I feel better for the exercise. Don't want to encourage her. She's too focused.

She changes her clothes and, just before she leaves, I hold her in my arms and kiss her warmly.

"Hey, are those tears I see in those eyes?"

"Nah, just an allergy attack. You better be here when I get back."

"Yes, boss."

I use some of that time studying the casino market in New England and New York to get an idea of the location of Royale's competition. There are seven casinos in New England other than the Royale. Full-fledged casinos are Lincoln, Rhode Island (Twin Rivers), Bangor, Maine (Hollywood Casino and Raceway) Oxford, Maine (Oxford Casino), and of course, Mohegan Sun and Foxwoods in Ledyard, Connecticut. In addition, two gambling facilities, one in Newport, Rhode Island (Newport Grand) and another in Plainville, Massachusetts (Plainridge Park) offer just slot machines. Lord, four more casinos have been licensed in the region and Newport Grand may be closed in exchange for a full casino in nearby Tiverton, Rhode Island. Thus, if everything that's been proposed materializes, these four New England states could be home to ten casinos and a slots parlor in five years. That's some dilution of the gambling dollar without even considering those in New York State. I could see that all this expansion could put enormous pressure on Roger's Casino Royale to stay profitable. I wonder if this would mean substantial reductions in personnel. If that happened, could it mean that some of the culprits would be cut loose? A lot of speculation, but my job is in the here and now, so I better get back to it.

Mr. Sam Lightfoot is the business at hand. I want to start nosing around into his background, but how would I do that without leaving telltale clues that could lead back to me? Should I wait until tomorrow to talk to Roger? Wake up Arnold, detecting is your business. Just tip toe around Mr. Lightfoot. I decide to start with my friend at the Motor Vehicle Department and dial her up.

CHAPTER V

"Hello, my name is Patrick Ingel. Is Sally Langone available?"

"Hold on Mr. Ingel, she is on the phone. I'll get her when she is finished if you can wait, or I can have her call you back."

"I'll wait a bit. Thanks." It was a short wait.

"Hi Patrick, are you calling to ask me out, I hope?"

"Oh love. I would do that in a second if I weren't so loaded down with work."

"Un, huh. Cut it out Patrick, I been snowed by experts. I'll get you in bed one of these days. What immoral and probably illegal act can I perform for you this time?"

"The immoral one must wait but the illegal one you can do as quickly as you can. It's the usual. A copy of a driver's license, in the name of Samuel Lightfoot."

"Middle initial?"

"None that I know of. But he probably lives in the Norwich/New London area. Or somewhere close by. Call me at this number when you find it and we will arrange a fax. Ok?"

"Sure, call you back within the hour."

Good as her word the phone rang twenty minutes later. It was Sally.

"Somebody has their wires crossed honey. We have no such listing in the files."

"Maybe I misspelled his name or maybe he has a middle initial."

"Nope. I already explored all these possibilities with our comprehensive software."

"Damn. I don't... wait a minute this is close to the Rhode Island and the Massachusetts borders. I assume you have reciprocal agreements with these two foreign states. Yes?"

"Of course we do, Mr. brilliant detective, but that will cost you extra. If I contact them, that means at least two dinners the very next time you are within a half hour of Hartford. Agreed?"

"You bet. And a shopping trip to the swankiest women's store in Hartford or West Hartford."

"Great, and you can help me pick out some fancy underwear or a slinky negligee, or both."

"It's a deal. Start calling. Bye."

I had been talking suggestive talk with Sally for several years. I am starting to think it is not all talk with her. Perhaps I'd better stop leading her on. Come clean about my recently acquired love. Perhaps she will stop trying to drag me into her bed.

About an hour passes before she calls back.

"Hello. Is this Sam Spade?"

"That's so funny Sally that I may die laughing."

"You could use a little humor in your life Patrick. You are always so serious. I hit pay dirt in Rhode Island and I hope none of my bosses will know about this transaction or I may be out of a job soon. You need any help on the project you are working on? I can retire with the full pension."

"I think my true love, Gineen and I can handle this job."

"Gineen, huh! I get the message. Give me a number where I can fax a copy of Lightfoot's license to you."

I give her the number of my fax machine back at the house and say to her, "Sally, no fooling around this time. You may have helped me crack this case and if that's how it plays out, you are in for a large, very large bonus. Thanks again. Take care."

I have some time before Gineen gets off work, so I drive to Cuprak Street for the fax of Lightfoot's license. The picture leaves no doubt that we have the right guy. We also have a street address in Norwich. Something to talk about with Roger tomorrow. I drive back to Gineen's condo just as she is driving up.

"Hey Mr. Detective, have you been out fooling around?"

"I was fooling around but it was not what you think."

I throw my arm around her shoulders and we walk inside. I give her a big hug and a kiss.

"Must be something very bad for you to try so hard to make light of it. Come clean."

"It's truly something big which you helped me get. Look here. This is a copy of Mr. Sam Lightfoot's driver's license. Cool, yes?"

"Very cool but how did I help? I never poached a driver's license in my life."

"Come on. Give yourself some credit. You got us his name and that's where this all started."

She takes a long look at the license I am holding up.

"Lesson number three in how to be a detective 101," I say. "I paid off a worker in the Connecticut DMV to get the license, as I have several times in the past."

"Oh, and how much do you pay this guy for a license?"

"In the interest of full disclosure, it's a woman. Normally I pay her $150 for a copy of a license, but in this case, because she had to contact the Rhode Island Department and because it's a key to our case, I told her she would get an extra-large bonus."

"And does this woman have nice large boobs, perhaps?"

"I wouldn't know, not ever having seen her in person."

"Really?"

"Really. But she has made certain overtures about meeting

for a drink, so you better behave yourself. I had thoughts about finding Lightfoot's house for a quick look, but that can wait until tomorrow morning."

"Good, I'll go with you."

"Come on, Gineen, this guy has lots to lose. Getting anywhere near him carries big risks."

"Good, I'll go with you."

I give up. This is one tough cookie I've latched onto.

"Ok, Miss Nancy Drew. You can go with me but remember he is dangerous and we are not going anywhere near him. Only want to catch a glimpse of his house. You got it?"

"Yep. Patrick, stop worrying about me. I've told you I am aware of the danger and I can take care of myself."

"Sure, but I can worry about my future wife, can't I?"

"You watch my back and I'll watch yours."

After breakfast the next morning, we drive to Enterprise Rental Car Company and rent a small economy sedan and then to the address on Lightfoot's license. We sit watching his house from a block away. I'm wearing dark glasses and a baseball cap to keep him from seeing me, should he pass our car. Sure enough, at 9:30 his garage door opens and out he comes, headed in our direction. As he passes us I get a glimpse of him while slouched down in my seat. Nice car, a Mercedes sports car. After he drives by us, Gineen says, "Boss I managed to get his license plate."

"Good job. Now we have his license, a photo, the make of his car and a license plate. A lot to talk to Roger about. Will you sit in with us? I want to suggest to him that you would be an asset he could trust as much as he could trust me."

"Sure."

We eat a quick lunch at a nearby restaruant. On the way out to the car, I say to Gineen, "I'm going to drop you off at your place and talk to Roger by myself. I want to ask him if it's ok for you to come over. Last time we talked, he was seriously pissed off at me for telling you anything about the job."

The drive to Gineen's and back to the house takes about 20 minutes. I gather together the information we have on Lightfoot and how we had obtained it. I'm making an outline when the doorbell rings announcing Roger's arrival.

"Come on in, Roger. I was just finishing some notes for you. Would you care for some tea?"

"Yes, I would. I am very tired. I have compiled the lists you asked for. Here they are. Please keep them in a safe place and don't show them to anyone. I have thought a lot about whether there are any employees or officials that I would trust to work on the inside. I'm not ready to say no, but as of this point I am loathe to assign anyone to do that inside work. Do you have a safe here that you could use to store these lists? No of course you don't, it was I who rented this place. I'll be glad when this problem is solved so I can get a few good night's sleep in a row. A couple of my employees have left because I had to cut back their hours as a result of the revenue decline. Everyone else, including me, is working longer hours to take up the slack."

"Thanks for the data. I think I will rent a safety deposit box at the bank to store them. I'll only take them out when I want to use them. I have what I think is good news for you. This may very well be a break in the case that leads us to the whole bunch of thieves."

"Tell me. I need good news."

"Here is a copy of Mr. Lightfoot's driver's license and here is a photograph of his house and car. Gineen and I picked up this data in the last few days and she was quick witted enough to get his license plate number."

"Did he spot either one of you?"

"Not a chance. He didn't even know we were there and wouldn't have seen our faces if he did. I even rented a car, so he wouldn't recognize mine or Gineen's."

"This is very good work Arnold. Should I ask how you got a copy of his license?"

"Not unless you really want to know. Rest assured there will be no feedback from my source. Before we go any further, I'd like to suggest we call Gineen over to listen to our plans because I believe she could be an asset in the investigation."

"I know your feelings about Gineen and I have to warn you that we are about to get into very dangerous waters. These people have much at stake and they will not hesitate to kill to protect their little scheme. The money they have stolen gives them the power to use any means they think they must to keep the money flowing. I don't doubt they will do that."

"Thanks for the warning Roger, but we have already discussed the dangers of being associated with this project. While I would prefer that Gineen stay out of it entirely, she is a tough cookie and is determined to help any way she can. Assuming, of course that you think it wise. One thing is certain. You can trust her to follow your direction."

"Ok. Let's call her and invite her over. I believe we will need all the trustworthy manpower we can find."

I get her on the phone. Tell her to come on over.

When she gets here, Roger lets her right in.

"Hi Gineen." He greets her with a big hug which really surprises me and her too, judging by the look on her face.

"Look, I have already talked to Arnold about the dangers of you getting involved with this project..."

"Roger, stop right there. I know this gentleman is really named Patrick Ingel and there is nothing about him that I don't already know. I know the potential danger of getting involved and I can promise you I will do nothing to endanger the investigation. You tell me what to do and I will do it. I love Patrick and when this is solved, which I know it will be, I hope he will ask me to marry him."

"And when you do, I expect to be at the wedding. In the meantime, I must warn you that I suspect our bad guys will stop at nothing to protect their scheme."

"I fully understand the risks, but I am determined to help in any way possible, unless you forbid it. I will respect your wishes. But every time Patrick goes out the door I will be left wondering if he will come back in one piece. Those feelings will be mitigated if I know what is going on."

"Then you both are on board. I hope that from this day forward you will be covering each other's backs. I must return to the Casino in about an hour, so we should do some planning about the next few days. Where do we go from here?"

"Roger, have you made up your mind about whether there is anyone on your staff that you can trust to work on the inside?"

"I've given that a ton of thought and at this point there isn't anyone I care to put on the job, inside or outside the Casino."

"Ok. Then think about this. Gineen is very bright as you probably have observed by now. She is a skilled conversationalist who makes perfect strangers comfortable talking to her. Finally, she has a degree in accounting from a college in Massachusetts, so she knows her way around money handling procedures and cash flow. She would be a perfect inside person if there is some way you can work her into the place."

"Now, wait a minute, you are asking me to do something I am not prepared to do. To be honest with you, I am having fatherly feelings about you both and that complicates my work tremendously. Don't ask me to do this."

"We are only asking you to consider it. It's the perfect solution to our problem of getting someone on the inside that we can trust. It's a logical next step. Think about it for a few days. In the meantime, I will be going over the records you have left me to see where that takes us. Ok?"

A grudging, "Ok," and he was out the door.

"An extremely nice man. We must really put the pressure on him, Patrick. From his all business veneer, I never would have guessed he had such a soft interior. What do you think he will do?"

"I believe he will put you in there. Let's face it, there is no other way. He has no choice. I can't go in and he can't do what needs to be done all by himself. You, my dear lady, are the only answer."

"I suppose if I was a truly honest person, I would tell you I am scared a little bit, but I will make myself forget that. I am looking forward to working on the problem and helping the both of you to solve it."

"A few days ago, I never would have thought you would be the key to this riddle, but you are. It may not scare you, but it scares me some. Don't forget, no matter what he decides you can always say no. If you don't mind, we have just enough time to make mad passionate love before you must be at work. Your place, it's safer. Race you there."

"You'll never beat me!" She punctuates this with a full fisted punch in the gut that all but disabled me.

She wins the race there by a mile. When we get inside I say, "That was unfair, you ruined my capacity to make love. Let's wait until you get off work. All that punching and tension."

"Not on your life, get up to the bedroom before I really work you over."

I do as I am ordered. Getting good at that. I don't regret it. The woman is incredible, and I feel so lucky to be with her. Never, ever have I felt this way before.

Afterwards, she tells me she must get to work. She will pave the way to leave the bar and get into her new job at the Casino.

Where, in the world did this woman get all her energy? I need to pay attention to her diet. Maybe I will learn something. I spend the next four hours going over the data that Roger brought me. It takes me that long to get a sense of some of the business cycles and then I fall asleep at the table.

"Wake up sweet man. I figured you had a long hard day, so I brought you some General Tso's chicken. Up to the bedroom but clean up this mess of papers first. I'll get into something more comfortable and wait for you. Make some tea, too."

"Hey, I thought you said you knew I had had a long hard day?"

"Stop whining or I'll get myself a real man."

I stop whining. I straighten all the papers up, make tea and warm up the General Tso. Then I bring the whole mess upstairs where Gineen is lying in bed watching the news.

"Here you are my queen, have at it while I go splash some cold water on my face."

We have a quiet night. After breakfast the next morning, I drag out the data that Roger has given me. I don't know if this will help any more now that Gineen is to be on the inside, but I think it's worth the effort. Some of this data might give her clues on what or who to watch.

The logical place to start is with Mr. Samuel Lightfoot. His initial job application tells me that he has been working at the Casino for about six months. He does not work in the accounting department or any cashier's location. No, indeed our man Lightfoot works in the parking garage. Interesting. This suggests that his role with the gang of thieves may be to act as an early warning system of some kind. Lightfoot had worked in an upstate New York casino prior to coming to Casino Royale. So, he has prior casino experience, but has been assigned to a nothing job. I make a mental note to ask Roger how and by whom employee assignments are metered out.

Next, I study the list of employees who handle the cash. These include the employees who physically handle and count the cash in the various cashier locations. That entire list amounts to about 50 people, some located on each floor of the Casino. There has been very little turnover of these employees, many of them having been hired years before. They, like all the workers, have been carefully vetted so that none were hired who had any criminal history. It's too soon to get any useful information from the list of employees by shift, so I put it aside for future use. A careful review of the revenue pattern doesn't turn up any absolute decreases in revenue, but it does show they leveled off about five weeks before I was hired and there has been very little revenue increase since. Of course, one explanation for the leveling off can well be the ever-increasing impact of competing casinos.

I make a note to ask Roger several questions:

1) Is there any chance that any of the employees could have been hired who have phony credentials?

2) Who on the staff is responsible for making job assignments? How long has this employee been on the staff?

3) How likely, in his view, would competition be responsible for the leveling of Casino revenue?

Gineen had hung around while I was studying the lists and occasionally looked over my shoulder and planted a kiss on the top of my head. After a while she comes into the room and announces she is going out to get her hair done. I stand and hug her and then walk her out to her car. I need the fresh air and indeed, it revives my tired brain. I decide to quit staring at the records for a while, make lunch and eat it slowly with a couple of beers. I need to stay away from the paperwork for a while, so I get in the car and drive to Mount Misery and climb to the top. Feels good. I'll tell Gineen when I see her. I'm certain she will be surprised considering how much bitching I did the first climb with her. It is a lot easier the second time. At the top I sit and take in the view for a while and then climb down the slope without incident, meaning I don't slip or fall once. Maybe there was something to this exercise business. When I get back to her place, I listen to music for a while and then watch part of a dreadful movie with Jennifer Aniston. I can't tell you the name because I turn it off and put it out of my mind. Back to reality with the 10 o'clock news, which I watch in the bedroom. I don't know when I fall asleep, but I wake up with Gineen standing in the bedroom doorway.

"You were sleeping soundly, and I tried not to wake you. Go on back to sleep and maybe we'll play a little bit in the morning."

This is one of the advantages of living with a woman who works in the evening. She turns out the light, sending me off to dream about climbing the Swiss Alps (in my bathing suit).

In the morning, I make an enormous breakfast while Gineen sleeps. She hops into the kitchen as I am wolfing down the last of my three eggs and corned beef hash.

"How do you do that without putting on an ounce of weight?"

"Easy. I exercise a lot."

"You do. When?"

"Well, like yesterday when I climbed up Mr. Misery."

"You didn't."

"Oh yes I did, and I felt great afterwards. I'm so glad I discovered that place."

"You're so glad that who discovered that place?"

"Oh yeah, you did. Thanks. I think the fact that I don't put on weight is simply due to my genes. All the members of my family are thin and some of them eat lots of dairy and other weight producing foods."

"It must have been close to dark by the time you got down to the bottom of Misery. Please be careful. I don't want you to do a humpty-dumpty. I haven't got time to put you together again."

"I promise, although I kind of like the idea of you putting me together."

"Funny. Please remember you are in the middle of a dangerous project. The bad guys could waylay you up there and hide your body where no one would find it for years, if ever."

"Good point. From now on I'll be packing when I go there."

"Better yet, I'll go with you and beat the crap out of anyone who tries to harm you. I'll need some energy to do a proper job of that so get me some oatmeal."

"Oh boy, a bodyguard who eats oatmeal. Am I lucky or what? Hey, I don't have anything to do before my meeting with Roger this afternoon so why don't we take a long walk around town? On the level."

"Sure."

After she eats the oatmeal, we leave the condo and walk for three hours. We must cover 20 miles. Part of the way we walk hand in hand, stopping from time to time to embrace like two young lovers.

"I look forward to the day when the project is over. We can do this every day like normal people, woman."

"Come on, Patrick, there will always be another project. Another mystery to solve and that my dear friend is your very own normal. After all, you are what you do and you, my friend, are a detective. There is no doubt in my mind that is what you always will be. This is what I bought with my eyes wide open."

"I suppose you're right. Will you be able to take that stress?"

"Absolutely, I will."

"And the children?"

"Hey, buster, we are not even married yet, so we'll work that out when we get there."

"You think a little practice in making babies would be in order right now? Like a dry run?"

"You bet. Let's get home. I don't want to practice in the street. Between your eating and your screwing, it's been a long day so let's get home. Maybe we can find time to try a bit of each."

We do just that and I can report directly from the playing field that practice went well and we are ready for the big game anytime. During lunch my throwaway cell rings. It's Roger.

"Arnold, I want to talk to you this afternoon around two o'clock."

"Ok, we'll be at the house waiting."

It's a few minutes before two by the time we finish lunch, clean up and drive to the house. Roger is sitting in his car waiting. When he gets out of the car, I notice he has a worried look on his face and I immediately start to wonder what terrible thing had transpired.

"Afternoon, you two. Let's get inside where we can talk."

Gineen leads the way into the house. As we enter I turn to Roger and ask, "What's happened? You look worried."

"Nothing has happened. Relax. I am just concerned about what I am going say to you. Just let me talk. I am ready to accept your idea to insert Gineen into the staff at the Casino, but I am plainly worried about doing that. At any time, if you change your mind about that, you must promise to tell me. We will find another way to solve our problem. If you would rather not go at all, simply say so now."

I look at Gineen and see the fire in her eyes. "If you're ready Roger, then I am too. To be fair to them, I need to give the G Bar a week's notice."

"Ok. Go ahead and give them notice today. After you get aboard we will give you about a week of training before you start to work. You will be paid for that, of course. In the meantime, Arnold and I will continue to look for additional ways to break this case wide open. Incidentally, this is not very important but, you can never be too careful. I notice that you have gotten in the habit of calling Patrick by his real name and I believe that it would be better to get used to calling him Arnold."

"I can see your reasoning on that, and it makes sense to me."

"I will call you tomorrow after you have found out when you will be leaving the G Bar. Promise me you will be extra careful. You won't take any risks that are not called for. And check with me if you think something unusual is called for."

"Roger, I can promise you that."

"Talk to you tomorrow. Goodbye."

I must admit that I feel somewhat uncomfortable. I realize that we were going to put Gineen inside that den of thieves. I have visions of all kinds of bad things happening to her. I'm not the only one. It was obvious that Roger has the same problem. A reflection of Gineen's charm, beauty and intelligence, I think to myself.

"Hey boss. What is that vacant look in your eyes?"

"Am I that transparent?"

"You forget, I read you like a book. Explain."

"I should know better than to hide anything from you. I was just getting cold feet. Your leaving the G Bar and going on board that leaky ship is bothering me. It was not much of a problem when the ship was way off on the horizon, but now that it's in the harbor, I see the reality of it. In short, I am scared for you."

"Who am I almost married to? Give me a hug cuz you are sweet. But buck up or I will knee you in the nuts."

"Thanks, Gineen for the hug. You have a way of making my troubles disappear with your warmth. Besides, I think you would really kick me and that might spoil the moment."

"You know I would, son. Now let me get off to the G Bar and break the news to them. See you when my shift is over. Make sure you are up."

"I'll be at the condo. See you there."

When she leaves, I make up mind that I need to do what I always do when I am in a funk. Well, when I'm not in a funk also. EAT.

I need a new place as a diversion and the Toshiba tells me to go to Illiano's Grill, a little farther away than my usual haunts, but not very far. It is in Yantic, which borders Norwich to the west. Illiano's turns out to be an overgrown Pizza Restaurant. I order Pollo Alla Francesa and Pasta Fagioli. Not bad for an Irishman. Gineen probably would not have approved. Sometimes eating by yourself is a good thing.

A full stomach goes right to my head and enables me to think about my meeting tomorrow with Roger. No fooling, there is a direct connection from my stomach to my brain. My list of items for discussion is short and after I have gone over it and outlined my own answers, I shift to the news and then a movie, Godfather I, for the 60th time. Another advantage of a bit of alone time. I never would have gotten that one past my love woman. I shut down the TV at 10:30, and fall asleep with the lights on. I dream I am with Sophia Loren. As I kiss her my eyes open. It is not a dream but the lips of Gineen.

"Sorry to wake you. Go on back to sleep. I'm going to take a shower and join you. Talk to you in the morning."

I am eating an early breakfast the next morning when Gineen comes into the kitchen, sleepily stretching her arms over her head. "Good morning, detective. I heard you rummaging around in here. Is there room for me?"

"Are you kidding? With a sexy nighty like that on, how could I say no?"

"Well, just say no until I take a shower. And then we'll talk."

"Ok. Can I fix you an omelet?"

"You bet. See you in fifteen."

Good as her word, she comes back into the kitchen as I am cleaning up my dishes.

"Sit my queen and I'll fetch you breakfast. I already have an omelet with cream cheese and blueberry jelly, warming in the toaster oven. Here's some coffee, and I'll make toast if you want."

"The omelet and coffee are enough. Sit while I tell you what went on last night. I talked to the owner of the G Bar last night. Told him that I had a very good job offer. Mmm, this omelet is delicious. He was very cordial. Said he didn't want to hold me back. He voluntarily arranged for someone to take over my job whenever I wanted to leave. As soon as tonight, if it would be helpful."

"You sure you didn't sleep with him?"

"Get out. He's ancient. Thirty-nine, I believe." (That's my age. Remember?)

Whack. Another closed fist to the shoulder. I am starting to anticipate what brings on these sudden punches. Now, all I need to learn is how to avoid them.

"I guess I asked for that, didn't I?"

"You certainly did. Anyhow I took him up on his offer. We can tell Roger that I'm available to start tomorrow morning. He even said that my job would be open for me, anytime I wanted to return. So great."

"And you're absolutely certain that you don't have to sleep with him?"

Before I can blink an eye she sands up, leans across the table and slugs me in the stomach, hard enough that I gag and almost lose my omelet.

"Jeez, Gineen, that hurt."

Looks like I still have a lot to learn about avoiding her wicked punches.

"Shut up and do my dishes. You earned that with your dirty mind. You know, not everyone thinks like you do."

"Just kidding."

She huffs out of the kitchen pretending to be angry. I know she's not. Or is she? I say nothing, figuring that I don't want to dig the hole any deeper. She's back in a few minutes with her street clothes on.

"Girl's got to dress for the job, creep. Gimme a check for $500, I'm going shopping."

What can I do? Why, give her the check of course.

"I'll be back before my new boss, Roger, gets here. See you."

CHAPTER VI

I do some more thinking about what I'm going to say to Roger. Three or four hours later, Gineen reappears with a ton of clothes that she unpacks and puts in her closet.

"Don't peek, creep. I'm going to put on some of my new clothes."

"I thought your old clothes looked pretty good. But, what do I know about women's clothes?"

"Nothing except how to take them off," she says with a little snicker.

Now, I am really digging it deeper. I shut up, sit down and wait. She starts the parade of smart looking outfits. I watch and nod approval at each one.

"Oh, lord you look great. The essence of the smart business woman. Good Job."

"You mean it or are you just kidding?"

"Certainly, I mean it. I am impressed. It's amazing how clothes can transform a person's persona. Well worth the $500. As you get more involved at the Royale, we will buy more. You will need them. And after all, it's Roger's money."

"Thank you dear. I'm glad I spent the money now. I know I'm ready for our meeting with Roger. I feel confident and ready to enter the big time. But still there is no need in over doing it."

We take our time with lunch and don't finish until about two. When he steps into the room, a big smile spreads across Roger's face. He steps back and admires Gineen. Ahem. It's like

I'm not even in the room. Hello there. Remember me? I am the detective.

"You look marvelous Gineen. The image of the competent business woman. I take this to mean that you are about ready to come to the Casino. Yes?"

"You got it. I had a very friendly meeting with the owner of The G Bar. He was pleased that I had a better job opportunity. He suggested he could arrange to fill my spot immediately. He didn't want to hold me up, even though I thought he was entitled to two weeks-notice. He was so insistent that I took him up on his offer and voila, I am ready to go to work as early as tomorrow morning."

"That's terrific. I'll need a day or so to make the appropriate arrangements. Let's meet back here tomorrow afternoon. You be ready to start as soon as the day after. Now Arnold, you have a paper with some notes on it. I take it you have some items to go over."

Finally, he remembers I am here. "I do. First, I am wondering if there is any likelihood that anyone on your staff could have submitted phony credentials?"

"I don't know. I suppose the correct answer to that is anything is possible. Let me think about that and you do the same. Right now, I don't see any way to even check on that with certainty."

"O.k. Second question. Do you believe that the increase in competition could account for the drop in the rate of increase of total revenue?"

"No, I don't. I don't believe that for a moment."

"Finally, who is responsible for keeping personnel records for your employees?"

"Why, that would be Emily Brown. She is the Personnel Director. She's been on the staff for several years. I do trust her. Well, that is, I always have trusted her. But now when I say things like that I must bite my tongue. Maybe, subconsciously, I just want to trust someone on the premises beside the other members of the Tribal Board."

"Does she also make recommendations to you for placing applicants and/or moving employees to different jobs?"

"Why yes. She does that frequently. I am beginning to see where you are going with this. We will do a little test when I submit Gineen's application."

"That's all I have. See you tomorrow."

Roger leaves and I look at Gineen.

"I think we are starting to make inroads toward a solution, love."

"I think you are right. We will make a good team. You on the outside. Me on the inside."

"*Miss Inside*. Suppose we attack Mount Misery this afternoon. I'm beginning to like the idea of some daily exercise. Maybe we should look around for a couple of bicycles, so we won't get bored with the same routine every day."

"Good idea. I'll make lunch and then we'll go. We could stop on the way back and look at bicycles.*"*

While she is making lunch, I drag out the Toshiba and search for a nearby bicycle shop.

"Lunch is served in the main dining room, partner. Did you find a good bicycle shop in town?"

"I did. The Rose City Bicycle Shop on Salem Turnpike which is not very far from here. They carry all the major brands and not only guarantee every bike they sell, but have a service shop on site. You know you can pay as much as $10,000 for a bike?"

"No, I didn't. I will stick with a heavy-duty mountain bike which shouldn't cost more than $500," she says.

"I doubt that we'll be doing any tooling around on mountain trails. I'll stick with a good 10 speed street bike."

"Thanks. And I'm still going to go for a mountain bike. You

do the dishes while I change into hiking friendly clothes."

She disappears for fifteen minutes while I wait. Raring to attack Mount Misery. Is this me? The wait is worthwhile. It's amazing how a woman in tattered shorts and sloppy sweat shirt can look so fetching. This time Mount Misery is a much easier and faster climb. Wonder of wonders, I get to the top before Gineen and must wait five minutes for her to catch up. I sit on a rock with a smug look on my face.

"Hey, Buster. Gentlemen usually wait for their lady friends and don't go running off. It's not a race you know. I slipped and started to slide back down the trail on a slippery rock. Look at all the scratches on my thighs".

"I'm sorry. You want Buster to kiss it and make it better."

"Knock it off, jerk face before I give you another fist in the stomach. And no, don't kiss them. I don't want them to become infected."

"That hurts. You know. I wish we lived closer to Mount Washington in New Hampshire. That's the highest peak in New England. That would be more of a challenge."

"You're kidding, right? Comparing this puny little hill to Mount Washington? The only way you would get to the top of that one would be to take the bus up the road or drive up the road yourself. The road is probably closed by snow and the only way you could get to the top would be by driving one of those big tracked machines they use. Then, when you got to the top you could enjoy 50 below temperatures, 200 mph winds and probably 50 feet of snow. You still want to be there?"

"Not so much. I'll remove it from the agenda, at least until the summer."

I start to speculate how it would feel making love on the top of this rock. Ok. I have a one-track mind, just like the Cog Railway on Mt. Washington and it works fine. I'll keep that thought to myself.

"I know what you are thinking, and the answer is no, it won't happen up here."

"Sure. We are connected. Are we not? You know sweet lady, while I was waiting here, I did some thinking about our assignment and I am almost certain that the key to cracking the case is Emily Brown, the personnel director."

"I knew from your conversation with Roger that's how you felt. Do you have any idea at this point what our next step would be in terms of getting the goods on her?"

"About the only way that I can see to start would be to backtrack into her past, before she went to work at the Casino. This could be time consuming and may not turn up anything. If I remember correctly, she came to the Casino from New York state which means some travel for me. I'd have to be very careful that she doesn't know that I am on her case. We'll go over this in some detail after lunch when we talk to Roger. Speaking of lunch, let's get back home and whip something up. All this exercise has made me very hungry."

"Really? I'd hate to think how hungry a real climb, like say Mount Washington, would make you."

"Oh, knock it off already."

I make lunch while she cleans up her scrapes and changes her clothes. Her shorts have taken a beating on her slide and probably are not repairable. Lunch is soup and salad with garlic bread. A bit on the light side for me but much to Gineen's liking, which is why I made it. Sort of a penance for abandoning her on the mount. We are ready and waiting for our two o'clock session with Roger, which I guess would be a critical juncture in our work. We will have to go on our bike buying trip later in the day or tomorrow. Promptly at two Roger knocks on the door.

"Hi Roger. Come on in, I'll make you some tea."

"Thank you, Gineen. I'd like that. Arnold. How are you?"

"Great"

"And you, Gineen?"

"Fit and ready to go to work. I've had lots of fresh air today on Mount Misery. That's good for the mind, but not so good for my butt which I scraped on a little fall."

"I may have to try that Mountain one day soon. Does your butt need any medical attention? We have an excellent medical staff at the Casino."

"No, it's not so bad that it won't heal by itself in a few days."

"Roger, have you found out anything about your personnel director Emily Brown? Is she married?" After all the talk about Gineen's butt I finally get into the conversation.

"Yes. She most certainly is, and her husband's name is Gordon. As nice a man as you would ever meet. I can't believe that either of these two could possibly be stealing from the Casino. But as we have found out, reality is not always what you think it is."

"You mean he works there?"

"No. He's a hard-working truck driver. Runs his own business, which I understand is very successful."

"Roger, I know you trust Emily, but at least give me some time to see what I can find out about the pair of them. I will be very discreet. They won't know that I am checking out their past life before they arrived in town. Maybe this is a wild goose chase. Sometime the people we trust the most are the ones we should trust the least. At best, I am only going to invest 3-4 days of my time and your money. If it's a dead end, so be it."

"Ok Arnold. You are the pro. Get right on it. Do you have a plan yet?"

"Well, just the beginning of one. I will start with their drivers' licenses and go from there."

"And how, pray tell will you get them?"

"It's better you don't know. Not always a good idea if my

clients get deeply involved with my somewhat shady investigative techniques."

"Ok. I get it. In the meantime, we will begin Gineen's training and familiarization at the Casino. Why don't we meet in four days and we will see where we are? Please let me know if you need more time. Goodbye."

"Bye, Roger."

After he leaves, I ask Gineen if she'd like to go bicycle shopping now.

"Why not? Then I'd have something to do if you take the next five days nosing around into Gordon and Emily's past life. Please stay away from the broad at the DMV, you hear?"

"That may not be possible. I may need her for license information."

"Get it over the phone."

I don't know what to make of this woman. She knows that I love her. I start to walk around the house. When I glance out a front window, I see a car parked at the curb directly in front of the house with two people in the front seat. I wonder if this is a security guard posted by Roger, so I get on the phone and call him.

"Sir, this is Kowalski. I am looking out the front window and I notice two guys in a large sedan parked at the curb. Have you posted security guards to watch over us?"

"No, not yet, but I have been considering just such a protective move."

"Oh, they are getting out of the car and approaching the house. Maybe I am being paranoid, but they have a sinister look about. Oh my God, they are the two brothers of the guy I shot outside the house in New Haven. Jesus. They are pulling guns..."

I drop the phone and rush to grab my gun from the bedroom. The best defense is an offense, so I fling open the front door and drop one of one of the two, before he has the presence of mind to react. Gineen screams.

The second brother turns and runs back to the car and races away. Once he started running away, I couldn't shoot him in the back. Maybe a big mistake. We'll see. The guy I downed is not making any sounds. When I hurry over to him, I can see he is dead. Within a few minutes, Rogers guards arrive. Roger must have sent them when I dropped the phone.

"Get back in the house, quickly. We'll handle it."

A few minutes later several police cruisers pull up with sirens blasting and lights flashing. I watch out the window. I see Roger's guards explaining to the cops that this is tribal ground and they will take over the investigation. One of the cops gets on his radio, apparently calling headquarters. After a minute or so, he holds up his hand, palms up. He is convinced, and the cops take off. Roger's guards clean up the mess.

In an attempt to distract ourselves from our brush with death, we go over to the bike shop and sure enough, Gineen ends up with a heavy-duty mountain bike while I am content to go with a light weight ten speed.

"So, Mr. detective, I suppose this means you will you will be playing with Sally, your old friend at the DMV. Yes?"

"Yes, I will but it only means a simple dinner out and a few hours to ply her with some wine."

"Just don't go any further than that, if you expect me to pay any attention to you when you get back. Make sure you just ply her and not play with her."

"All in the name of advancing our work, hon. Relax. We are good and always will be."

"A bike ride before dinner?"

I wanted to say no, but how could I do that without appearing to be the wimp that I was? Sometimes it's not any fun having a girl friend who performs like an Olympic athlete.

"Sure. maybe a short ride, like to the gas station and back."

"Follow me," she says.

So, I do. She literally runs out the door and hops on her monster mountain bike and heads for the open road. For all I know we will be riding all the way to Hartford and back. Or maybe Chicago and then I would miss dinner. She quickly puts a substantial distance between us. I am wondering if this is payback for not waiting for her on the climb up Mount Misery. Soon she is out of sight. I push hard to catch up. I eventually do and there she is, sitting on a rock sunning herself. I expect some sarcasm and I am not disappointed.

"Were you riding the bike or walking big strong mans?"

"Funny. Come on, we passed a hot dog stand back toward the house. I'll buy you a hot dog or even a hamburger."

Before she can tell me that we are not finished with the ride, I hop on my ten-speed, and start back toward home as fast as I can. Of course, she passes me in five minutes and is already munching a cheeseburger and French fries when I get to Hamburger Heaven. I get the snicker I expected and then order a hotdog and a coke. When we have eaten, she puts her arm around my shoulders and whispers in my ear, "Head home baby and see if you have anything left in the tank. We'll ride side by side as we will for the rest of our lives."

So, this really was a lesson in retribution. Ah well, maybe I deserved it. Back at the condo we embrace, and I suggest that we order Asian food delivered and watch a movie later while we eat dinner. The afternoon is spent puttering around and doing mundane household chores. I pack some clothes for tomorrow's trip. I am growing into a wimp because I don't like the prospect of leaving this beautiful creature for 5 days. But work is work. It was my idea. Wasn't it?

"Good idea. I suggest General Tso's chicken without the hot peppers, spring rolls, chicken wings and steamed veggies. You call while I slip into something more comfortable."

I call in the order and they tell me it will be delivered in about 30 minutes. I hang up. Hearing the shower going I shed my clothes and join Gineen there. Turns into the best shower I ever had. The doorbell rings just as I finish dressing and it's our food. Excellent timing. The food is great, as is the company, of course.

"Gineen, I have an idea. Instead of a movie let's listen to music."

"I like that. I'm in the mood for something retro."

"Fine with me."

That's how we spend the rest of the evening, resting on some pillows in front of the fireplace, munching on Asian Cuisine and listening to Frank Sinatra, Dusty Springfield, and many others including Louis Armstrong. At the end of a perfect evening I turned to Gineen and after nibbling on her ear for a bit, I whisper, "Let's just spend the night right here."

"You are reading my mind."

We fall asleep right there and don't wake up until the fire is nearly out. Off to bed for the rest of the night.

After breakfast, we both leave the condo heading in opposite directions; she off to the Casino to start her training and me off to the west to find out what I could about Emily and Gordon Brown. That means a stop in Hartford to see my favorite DMV clerk, one Sally Langone. Before I get there, I call her on my cell.

CHAPTER VII

"DMV, Sally Langone."

"Patrick Ingel, Private Investigator. How's the best-looking government employee in the entire state? Maybe the entire country."

"Aw stop, you make a girl blush. You are coming for a date. Right?"

"Sally, you deserve better than me."

"That's a no, right? Scorned, again. What's a girl got to do to the snare a big good-looking guy like you? What's up Sherlock?"

"Why don't we talk about it at lunch?"

"Can't do that. I am in danger of having my little enterprise exposed, so I'm trying to be very discreet. We can talk over dinner at my place."

I want to say no, but if I want to get anything out of her there doesn't seem to be any alternative.

"Ok, where do you live?"

"I live in West Hartford. Say about seven o'clock. You bring dinner. Here's the address."

She hangs up after giving me her address, but before I can give her the names of the Browns. Probably intentional. She seemed genuinely worried about someone exposing her little extra-curricular business, so I don't call back. What the hell, I'll find out tonight. With luck, she can gather the information I need in the morning and if all goes well, I'll be on my way without staying overnight again. I walk around downtown

Hartford touching all the places I could remember from previous visits including the State Capitol. I have lunch at the Franklin Giant Sandwich Shop and then do some more walking. I want to get on with my background search of the Browns, but I am totally dependent on Sally for driver's license information. At about six thirty, I stop at a nearby Asian restaurant and load up with two large take-out bags filled with every Asian dish I can think of. I ring her doorbell promptly at seven. I can hear her approach the door, and I sense she is checking me out through the little peep hole. Locks click open. A safety chain is released as the door opens. There she is in all her splendor, dressed in a slinky little thing which was more suitable for sleeping than dining. Sally has been putting the make on me now for several years, but I have deliberately stayed away. Time and again I have tried to convince her I was a "taken man" to no avail. Not a good idea mixing business with pleasure. I have a rule about that. Too bad because I came close several times before I had Gineen.

"Come on in Patrick. God, are you expecting another dozen people to join us and eat all that food?"

"Nah. Always nice to have left over Asian food in the fridge. I sometimes eat it for breakfast."

"Good. You can eat some of it in the morning when I wake you. I leave here at seven, so you better be up," she says with a little glint in her eyes.

"Sally. I can't think of anyone I'd rather spend the night with, but I can't. I am engaged to be married (a small exaggeration) and being unfaithful would be bad way to start out. Please understand."

"I do but you must excuse me if I forget occasionally. Now that I see you in the flesh, I am even more attracted to you."

"Thanks for the compliment, Sally. I sense there are other reasons for not getting together for lunch. Are there?"

"Indeed. I find that my bosses are keeping a very close eye on me and I don't know why. I hope they are not becoming aware of my little business. I can't stop worrying they are waiting to pounce at any moment. I am making it a point to meet my customers in private, after business hours. Of course, I only wear this outfit for one special guy. Let's go into the dining room and attack all that food."

Once she understands that I won't cheat on Gineen, we both relax and enjoy a great dinner. Over coffee, I outline my mission to her.

"I am working for a gambling casino in Connecticut that is experiencing a substantial and continuing theft of its revenue. Please understand this is highly confidential, so not a word to anyone."

Given her worries about her bosses, I don't expect any problem with her talking to anyone about me.

"Pardon me for interrupting but that involved a guy by the name of Lightfoot that you asked me to get a license for. Didn't it?"

"You have a good memory and that was very helpful information. We have him under surveillance. But the mission I am pursuing just now involves two other people who apparently moved here from New York State. I need license information for them, so I can find their former New York address. I'm essentially snooping around into their activities before they came to the Casino. They are a married couple by the names of Emma and Gordon Brown. Whatever you can get me on them will be appreciated. I can tell you that this case is worth big bucks to the Casino and to me. I promise your help will result in a very large bonus for you."

"Well that won't compensate for losing access to you, but it will ease the pain, Patrick. I will check out these two people as early as I can in the morning and call you on your cell. In the meantime, if anything gets in the way with your new honey, just know I am standing by."

"Ok. Talk to you in the morning."

I find a motel nearby and check in for the night. I call Gineen on my cell. She answers right away.

"Hello."

"Good evening love of my life. How are you?"

"Lonely, what do you think?"

"Me too. I am at a motel near West Hartford and I won't get anything out of Sally until tomorrow at the earliest."

"So, you've talked to her already?"

"Yes. I did."

"Are you going to tell me what went down, or do I have to drag it out of you piece by piece?"

"I just finished dinner at her place and I won't get any information until tomorrow, so I've checked into a motel for the night."

"What there are no restaurants in Hartford?"

"She is nervous about meeting any of her customers in a public place because she thinks her bosses might be getting on to her shady business dealings. She suspects they are looking for ways to catch her with the goods. I admit I had to fight her off at first until I told her I was engaged. She backed off, then."

"Engaged, are we? Or is that with another woman that I don't know anything about?"

"Gineen, dammit, you promised!"

"Sorry. Go ahead."

"Well, she promised to try and get the data I need sometime tomorrow. She must do it surreptitiously, when her bosses aren't around. I suppose that means at lunch time or after work. I don't really know when I will get it, but it could mean another night here before I can get going. I hope not."

"Ouch. I knew you'd be gone for a few days, but it starts to look like an extended period. I miss you and I'm sorry for all the sarcastic remarks and innuendos. Get some sleep and call me when you know something. Good night and I love you dearly."

"I will call you the minute I know anything. Good night, love of my life. I miss you."

When I hang up I realize how much that woman means to me and how much I don't like being separated from her. I watch a bit of useless television and then spend a restless night. I finally fall sound asleep near 5 am. I shut off my internal alarm clock since I had absolutely nothing to do at least until lunch time. I wake up at 10. By the time I have showered, dressed and eaten breakfast, it is twelve thirty. The cell rings a few minutes later and it's Sally.

"Ok Sherlock, get a pencil and make some notes. Your couple both had New York driver's licenses with the following address; 106 Ellen Avenue in Niagara Falls. If I had some more time I would have searched the internet to see what else I could learn about them. Since you are a detective, you can do the same searches. I assume you have your computer with you."

"I do. Never leave home without it. Thanks so much, Sally. I owe you a big one."

"I won't touch that with a ten-foot pole. You're welcome and good luck up there."

Oh hell, I was in for a long drive. I throw my clothes together and consult Toshiba for the best routes. Going west from Hartford is possible only through a maze of state roads. The fastest way was north on Interstate 91 toward Springfield, Massachusetts and then west on the Mass. Pike all the way into New York State and across the Hudson, just south of Albany. It would probably take the rest of the day and part of tomorrow, Friday. When I get on the Mass Pike, I pull into the first service area for gas and to call Gineen. No answer on her cell so she was probably busy getting started on her training. With all the traffic, it takes me about two hours to reach the bridge across the Hudson River where I pick up Interstate Route 87 north around Albany. Since it will be another four and a half hours driving time to Niagara, it makes sense to stop overnight. I get off the Interstate and check into a motel. I don't look forward to another boring evening, but I am tired and there is no sense pushing myself. I ring up Gineen after a mediocre meal at a nearby restaurant.

"Gineen Walker."

"No kidding. And this is Arnold. How was your day?"

"Hey, my day was long and tiring. Lonely without my true love. Where are you now, love? On your way home?"

"I am at a motel just outside of Albany. Driving is not my thing and it tires me out more than anything else I do."

"And do our friends come from the Albany area?"

"No, they don't. They come from Niagara Falls which is where I'm headed tomorrow. Too bad you're not along, we could get married there. Have a honeymoon up there like a lot of people do."

"The very thought of that makes me a little weepy. I wish we could."

"I promise you we will do just that when this job is done. And maybe on to Honolulu. Who knows where else?"

"If I ever wanted this search to be successful and over with, I do now with every bone in my body."

"Get some rest Gineen and I will call you tomorrow evening about this time. Good night, love."

"Good night Arnold."

Another restless night.

I wolf down a humongous breakfast of corned beef hash and eggs with home fries and a bucket of coffee. No matter what is going on, my appetite is always good. I take in enough fuel to keep me going until I get to Niagara Falls for a late lunch. Back onto Interstate 90 all the way to Buffalo and then north to Niagara Falls. The Sheraton on the Falls Hotel looks like a good bet. I am going first class because I figure I will be in town for at least a couple of days and I need as much comfort as possible. I have no worry about my staying here being an issue with Roger. He believes in going first class. After breakfast, I start the search at 310 Fourth Street, the address on their NY driver's licenses. That address turns out to be a small apartment building with six units. I don't expect anyone to be at home at this hour, but I start the search with a knock on the door of apartment 3, which was listed on the license. Just as I expected, there was no answer. As luck would have it, the door of the next apartment opens. An elderly woman comes out into the corridor and approaches me.

"They are not at home, young man. Can I help you with anything?"

Young man? Oh, that's me. "Well, actually I am trying to find the previous tenants in this apartment, the Browns."

"Well, if you know they are not there anymore, why are you looking for them?"

I hesitated momentarily. I didn't know how far to go with this woman. Instinct tells me to trust her.

"To be honest with you, I am a private detective and my client wants to find the Browns."

"Why so, sonny?"

"He thinks they have kind of a shady background. He is worried they may try to harm him and his business."

"That so? Where you from?"

"Well that's confidential information and I don't think my client would want me to disclose any more information about myself or him."

"Alrighty. You have an honest face. What can I tell you?"

I have an honest face. What does that look like?

"Anything you might know about the Browns."

"I don't know much. They weren't very friendly people."

"Do you happen to know when they left or where they worked? Or anything else that could be helpful in finding them."

"There was something mighty suspicious about them all along. Particularly the way they left, and all. One night, they just up and went. Took their clothes and left everything else. The landlord just threw it all in the trash. It was a few months ago. As far as I know they both worked at the Casino Niagara. But I ain't sure about that."

"I certainly thank you for this information. You have been very helpful. Let me leave you a card with my cell phone number on it in case you think of anything else. Oh, before I leave, could you look at these pictures on their driver's licenses, just to make sure these are the two that lived here?"

"That's them, alright."

"Thank you again. Good bye."

"Good bye and good luck. I never liked them two. I always knowed there was something bent about them."

Next stop for me is the Niagara Falls police station. I find it easily and stride up to the desk sergeant and show him my card.

"I am working on an out of town case and would like to talk to the chief if he is available."

"Certainly. Can I tell him what you would like to talk about?"

"It's a confidential matter and I would like to talk to him first. Let him decide who else I should talk to."

That draws a quizzical and alarmed look to his face. Nevertheless, he responds, "O K. Have a seat and I'll tell him you are here. Be right back."

"Thanks."

I walk around the outer lobby for ten minutes checking out a bulletin board that has a series of complimentary newspaper clips on it and some "wanted" photographs. Mostly for minor crimes in both cases.

The chief comes out and greets me with a hearty, firm handshake.

"Come on into my office. Have a seat." He sits down at his desk, which looks organized and workmanlike. "What can I do for you?"

"Well, I am investigating a theft case for a client in Connecticut that I believe involves a couple who used to work at the Casino Niagara."

"Hold on a minute, their names wouldn't happen to be Brown, would it?" A light goes on in his eyes as he blurts this out.

"Why yes, that's them. Have you had some contact with them?"

"All I know is that they skipped town leaving a substantial unpaid lease on their apartment. I know that because their landlord called me on it. We looked around town for them but could not find a trace. So, we gave up on it. That was some months ago, and I assume they left town for places unknown, probably far away."

"I understand they worked for the Casino. Wouldn't they have asked you into the case, if there was a case?"

"You do know that American Indian Casinos are on sovereign land over which we have no oversight, unless they ask for help. We have a good working relationship with the Casino, but they did not ask for help on that one. I suggest that you talk to the general manager, Manly Sand. If you want, I can call over there and get you an appointment whenever it's convenient for the two of you."

"Thanks chief. That would be helpful."

"Wait a second."

"He dialed a number."

"Hello Manly. This is Chief Stevens. I have a Private Investigator in my office. He's working on an out of state case and would like to talk to you. Seems like a straight guy. Ok, I'll tell him."

"He says he can see you tomorrow at lunchtime at the Casino. I thought that would be ok with you."

"It's fine. That'll give me some time to relax in the morning and maybe do some sightseeing. I would like to thank you very much for your help."

"Well, I didn't do much. Good luck on you search. Take care."

I leave the station and drive back to the hotel. Given that I won't see Hand until lunch tomorrow, I figure I may be here, or somewhere close by at the end of the day tomorrow. Another evening without Gineen but at least this is more interesting than a motel off the Interstate. I clean up and go into the cocktail lounge for a few drinks and then into the restaurant for a delicious rib eye and baked potato. I spend another lonely night, watch another silly movie and then call Gineen. I sleep like a baby until seven the next morning. From what I can remember babies don't sleep that well. I wonder where that saying came from. Anyhow, I eat a late breakfast at the hotel and then go sightseeing. I suppose I see most of the usual tourist spots. In the process I get some badly needed exercise from a lot of walking. I go to the Casino well before lunch time and walk around the place. It's a learning experience. What I learn is that if you have seen one casino you have seen them all. The size and shape vary, sure. But the slots and table games look the same as do the customers striving to beat the system. At 12 noon, I find Sand's office. Interesting.

The name plate on his door reads *Dr*. Manly Sand. I go in and am greeted by a beautiful young woman who asks me to take a seat while she gets the good Doctor.

CHAPTER VIII

"Dr. Sand, pleased to meet you. Chief Stevens says nice things about you."

He walks into the reception area a few minutes later, extends his hand and shakes mine firmly. He is thin and wiry.

"Drop the doctor. That's an adornment that I could do without even though the training comes in handy at times."

"If it's not too personal what kind of medicine did you practice?"

"None. I have a PHD in psychology. Helps dealing with the customers at times."

"Based on my limited experience, I can understand how that training might come in handy, frequently."

"Mr. Kowalski, I don't mean to rush you, but I do have some State officials coming in about an hour. What can I do for you?"

"First, I will ask that whatever I tell you can be kept confidential. Our problem is in the early stages of investigation. It is likely some internal staff members are stealing some cash at our casino. We would like our conversation to be kept confidential so the bad guys don't go underground."

"That goes both ways and I have no problem with it."

"Ok. To start out, Kowalski is an assumed name. My real name is Patrick Ingel. My client on the case I am working on is named Roger Jones, who manages the Casino Royale in Connecticut. He strongly believes that one, or more likely several employees, are stealing large amounts of cash."

"Let me interrupt you. What do you mean when you say that he believes that theft is going on?"

"As far as we know, the thieves are covering up the theft by manipulating the books. Based on an analysis we are almost 100% sure that this has been going on for an extended period. It's difficult to estimate, but the losses are large. Certainly, in the many millions. We suspect that the Casino's personnel director, Emily Brown, and her husband are involved. I have backtracked them here to the Falls and I wonder if they worked at your casino or some other one in the area?"

"Indeed, they did, for a period of several years. While they were here, we experienced the exact same problem you are having now. It took us that long to discover they were thieves. By then, they somehow figured out that we were on to them and disappeared without a trace. Understand, it would have been a major embarrassment to the Casino had we made the problem public, so we kept it quiet. We still don't know how much they made off with, but it was assuredly in the millions of dollars. I would suggest that however you treat the problem don't let them know that you are on to them because they appear to be set and ready to disappear at a moment's notice. They have perfected the art of quickly disappearing in addition to their success at stealing."

"The first thing the Casino did was to hire me, an outside investigator. No one at the Casino knows about me except for the manager. We then planted a woman into the Casino's accounting and auditing staff just about the time I left to come up here. She is an experienced accountant. It is our hope that she will be able to identify all the members of the gang, so we can pounce on all of them at the same time and throw them in jail for a long time. We already know one of the members of the crew and have had him under surveillance."

"Well detective, it sounds like you are proceeding just as we should have. I do feel somewhat responsible for letting them get away, so they could plunder your casino. If there is any way that I can help please, let me know."

"No apology necessary. I feel confident that the whole gang we are dealing with did not come from here. If all goes well, I'm sure you will have an opportunity to help send them to jail. I haven't discussed this with my client, but if we recover any of the stolen money, we will return any portion of it that can be traced to your casino."

"That would be fine but sending them to jail would be payment enough."

"Good enough. I'll get out of the way and let you get ready for meeting with the State officials. Thanks again for your help."

"No. Thank you for coming. Good luck with your investigation and have a safe trip home."

It was now one o'clock. Too late to drive all the way home but if I start today, it will shorten my drive tomorrow and get me home in time to meet Gineen when she gets through at the Casino. I go back to the Sheraton and check out. I am going home armed with ammunition for Roger and the Royale. I can't think of any more work I could do here, so I hit the highway. I drive until five and then get off the Interstate and find a motel near Albany, that has a diner nearby. At five fifteen I call Gineen and get her voice mail. I leave word that I am on the way home and would she call me on my cell. After cleaning up, I hit the diner for dinner and am just starting my meal when the cell phone rings.

"Good to hear that you are finally coming back to the one who loves you. Where are you?"

"I'm in a diner just outside of Albany catching a bite."

"Well nothing new there. Are you coming home tonight, or do I have to spend another night in a cold and lonely bed?"

"Too tired to do that. I'll be on the road early tomorrow and will probably be back in town by lunch. I want you to set up a meeting with Roger after work tomorrow at the usual place. You can tell him it was a very successful trip and I expect him to be happy with the results."

"He may be happy, but I am very unhappy about spending another night by myself. Please be prepared for a long drawn out welcome home. Get a good night's sleep tonight because you won't be getting much tomorrow night. We have a lot of catching up to do. And bring me flowers and champagne. Now finish your dinner before it gets cold."

"Ok, boss. See you then. No long meeting with Roger, tomorrow. We can do that the day after. Goodnight."

"Hey, you be kind and respectful to Roger. After all, he's our meal ticket."

"I will, but he knows us well enough to understand that we need some quality time tomorrow night. And anyway, I guarantee you that he will be overjoyed with the results of my trip. I am seeing the light at the end of the tunnel. Goodnight."

I eat dinner with gusto, buoyed by the feeling that we are finally making some progress. I go back to the motel where I spend another restless night. I really do love that woman and I have been away from her far too long. Despite the restless night, I manage to find my way back to the diner for a mediocre breakfast. I go light on the coffee because I am starting to notice it is producing some reflux. Maybe I will switch to tea. Ugh, what is happening to me? I get on the road early for an uneventful drive home. I get back early in the afternoon and take a nap before Gineen and Roger arrive. She pops in the door at five thirty. I greet her with a long hug and kiss.

"It's good to be back where I belong, here in your arms. I missed you terribly. Let's grab a quickie."

"Don't be silly, Roger is right behind me and we need to talk about your findings. Besides you don't get away with any quickie. Be prepared for a long sleepless night."

"Like I said on the phone, a short meeting is ok but the rest of it we can do tomorrow. You look and taste smashing good. Is that one of your new business outfits?"

"Yes. You like?"

"I like it. I hope I don't damage it when I rip it off your lovely body later tonight."

Sure enough, Roger's knock on the door comes five minutes later.

"Come on in Roger."

"Welcome home, Arnold. Gineen tells me you come with good news."

"Come on in and get comfortable." I get a hardy handshake and a pat on the back before I can open my mouth.

"Let me summarize. My suspicion about your personnel director is dead-on correct. She and her husband lived in Niagara Falls, New York before they came here. I talked to the General Manager of the casino there, in strictest confidence and he admitted that they both worked at the Niagara Casino and stole a pile of money before he found out. They escaped town before he could round them up. Until I told him, he had no idea where they had gone. He seemed to think they had just retired and taken their loot to some warm far off place. I suppose that once a thief, always a thief and there never is enough. So, essentially that is the news."

"Patrick, you have done an excellent job. Everything I heard about you before I hired you has come true. I am overjoyed at your news, but I must say that I embarrassed by it because I trusted Emily like she was a member of the family. I feel like there is no one at the Casino that I can trust, save for Gineen."

"Roger, don't feel bad. She is a professional liar with years of practice. She fooled Manly Hand at Niagara and he has a

PhD in Psychology. Besides, it feels like we are making good progress".

"Now that we know this key link to the gang of thieves, our next step should be to develop a plan to catch them all and throw them in jail. After all we still need evidence, be it in a Tribal Court or the town's Criminal Court."

"I agree, but I am much too tired to do any thinking about that tonight and I need to spend some time with Gineen. I hope you understand."

"I understand that. You have done an excellent job so take as much time as you need. I will leave that decision in your capable hands. But don't keep Gineen away from the Casino for more than a day. She is learning fast and I don't want the staff members to wonder where she is. Gineen, I suggest you call in sick tomorrow."

"I'll do that boss, and thanks for understanding. Good night."

"Good night kids." He is quickly out the door.

"Did he say kids?"

"Come on Patrick. You must know by now that he looks at us as the kids he never had."

Not very long after we hear his car leave, we are at each other in a flash and make frantic love right there in the living room. Then we have an encore in the bedroom which is slow and less urgent. Outside a few whispered expressions of love, we are silent. No need for words, the actions speak very loudly. I don't know when we fall asleep, but I do know that our bodies are still entwined. I do love this woman. I love her even more when the smell of coffee comes wafting into the bedroom from the kitchen early next morning.

"Gineen, you don't have to do this. It's becoming a habit. You don't mind if I eat in my jammies before I even shower, do you? You don't know how good it feels to be away from crummy diner food at last."

"I do have to do this. I want to do it every day for the rest of our lives. And you can eat bare ass naked, if you like. In case you hadn't noticed, this is your favorite breakfast, corned beef hash and eggs."

It is by far the best breakfast I have ever eaten. While the food is delicious, there is nothing unusual about that. No, it is the company and an overwhelming feeling of well-being that does it.

"Have I told you yet this morning that I love you?"

"Yes, you did, but I will never get tired of hearing it. A nice diamond would help too. But even that doesn't relieve you of the duty of doing the dishes. Go to it while I shower and get ready to spend this day with the man of my dreams."

I struggle through the dishes, never my favorite assignment, but I do as I was ordered. Upstairs I start to take off my jammies just as she is coming out of the shower.

"Yum, just in time. We don't have anything we need to do this morning so why don't we try an encore?"

"Go shower and brush your scuzzy corn beef teeth and we'll talk."

"Talk was not exactly what I had in mind."

"Go."

That sounds like an order so into the shower I go. When I finish, she is fully dressed and ready to go. Somewhere. Ugh. To go hiking. At least that is what it looks like based on the shorts and hiking boots.

"As if I don't know; what is on your agenda?"

"Mount Misery, so I don't run into Brown or one of her cohorts."

"I'm sorry but that was not the kind of exercise I had in mind. We could avoid her by hiding in the bedroom all day."

"It's obvious what you had in mind. Put on your little boy

pants and let's go. Save what's on your mind for later. Dinner, flowers, a movie, and love. Sound good?"

"I can't turn down an offer like that, but you don't really have to buy me flowers and wine."

"Funny."

We drive out to Mt. Misery and by the time we get there, the weather is perfect. No competition going up the trail. Each of us looking out for the other. At the top, we sit and sun ourselves and smooch a little. We stretch out and sleep a bit. Imagine sleeping on a rock mattress. A small clicking wakes me. It 's Gineen with her camera, taking pictures of me.

"Hey, stop with the pictures and let's go down. It's almost lunch time let's get going."

"Sit back and relax."

She started emptying out her backpack. First a table cloth, next plastic silver ware, drinks and small sandwiches. We eat lunch on the rock and then return home. And then off to sleep, contented as a lamb.

With all this quiet time, I start to get a bit antsy the next morning. I make breakfast. Do the dishes as well.

"Wife. I hope you don't mind, but I've got to start doing something today or I will go batty."

"I understand because I am having some of the same feelings myself. I guess there is a limit to the number of hours that one can eat, screw, and sleep without looking for some work to do. Do you have something in mind?"

"The only thing I can think of is some surveillance on the house of Sam Lightfoot. Not a very inviting bit of detecting and will probably turn up nothing, but I think I'll try it for a few hours."

"You're not thinking of trying to get into his house, are you?"

"Nope. Just sitting in the car and watching the outside for

any unusual activity. The bane of most private detectives. What are you up to today?"

"I'm thinking that I'll go to the Casino and do some scheming about things I should be doing on the inside. Employee shift assignments, days off and the like. You aren't the only one who can play detective."

"While you are at it, pay particular attention to Lightfoot's and Gordon Brown's schedules. They are the only two working outside the walls of the Casino. I don't think that Emily would be getting her hands dirty, but those two might be. Or maybe you might turn up a lead on any other members of the gang."

"Ok. Good Idea. I will go into the Casino and tell Emily that I am feeling better. My training schedule just moved to her office, so I can get access to those records, if Roger can distract her for a while with other business."

"Good. I don't suppose I need to tell you that we ought not be calling each other. Save whatever you learn until we get back here."

"Let's go. It feels good to finally have some leads to follow up. See you later."

"Ok. Just be careful."

At Lightfoot's house, I park about a block away where I can see anyone coming into or going out of the front door. There is no place where I can see the back door, if there is one. Nor can I see the door to his garage. There is very light traffic on the street, but I am only visible from a few of the houses. I figure I can probably stay in place for a couple of hours before I have to move. Shortly, a car pulls into the driveway. A man gets out and walks to the front door and rings the doorbell. In a minute the door opens, and he steps inside. I assume it's Lightfoot who lets him in, but I can't see him. I move the car closer to the house after a few minutes to a spot where I should be able to see the guy when he comes out. He is in there for fifteen minutes and when he comes out the door, I slowly drive by, so I can get a quick look at his face. *Jackpot*. Gordon Brown. Nothing more to be learned here so off I go back home. Gineen is not home yet so I make myself a light lunch and read some of the local papers that have backed up the days I was traveling. Nothing new there so I turn on my Kindle and start to read the mystery novel that I bought recently from Amazon for 99 cents. Gineen arrives shortly after five thirty. After a hug, she looks at me and smiled.

"You found something, didn't you?"

"How'd you know?"

"Can tell by the look on your face. Tell me, I can hardly wait. It's something meaningful. I can tell."

"It certainly is. I spotted Gordon Brown visiting the Lightfoot place, so we now have another lead that is an important link."

"Maybe, but by itself it is of little value as evidence. Isn't it?"

"No. Of course not, but it's another step down the trail. Roger may want to pursue it further, maybe by hiring another P.I. to track Brown. Do we even know where he lives?"

"I'm not sure., I only assume he lives with Emily. I can certainly find that out with little trouble."

"Gineen, do we even know for a fact that they are married?"

"I guess not."

"We're doing a good job of raising questions. That's a start, but we really need to wait to sit down with Roger and dope out a plan. But I feel good about our recent progress. We've made a good start along this road. And I think we will be successful. I have all of tomorrow to noodle around, now that you have 'recovered' from your illness. It would be good if you could put together a list of all the employees in the accounting department. It's safe to assume that at least one of them is a member of the gang. Yes?"

"Absolutely. There has to be a gang member working there and covering up the thefts by under reporting the take."

"I'm worn out from thinking and speculating about this undertaking. I propose we pack it in for the evening. How about dinner and a movie?"

"You're on. Who's cooking?"

"Whoever is working at the Pizza Shop. I'll call while you search Netflix and pick out a chick flick that I can tolerate."

"I was thinking *The Godfather*, wise guy!"

"Pizza and *The Godfather* in the same day? Are you ok?"

"I'll add some Tofu to my half of the pizza, so it will be ok."

" When the Pizza God hears about that, he will be angry."

The pizza is delivered about 40 minutes later and I'll be dammed if she didn't really stick little cubes of Tofu on her half of it. No word from the Pizza God yet. And wonder of wonders we really do watch *The Godfather*, which is one of my favorite movies and one of her least favorites. Maybe this is a trap I am headed into. Her slave for a year or something like that. Nothing wrong with that. When the movie is over, she looks at me with a cunning smile on her face.

"What next, Sherlock. How do we end this perfect evening?"

"What I am wondering is how many times we can have sex between now and noontime tomorrow."

"Care to venture a guess? Maybe the one who guesses correctly gets a prize."

"You mean like a box of cigars and two tickets to next week's show? I'll say three times."

"You are going to lose this one. Five times would be more like it. If you can't do that, I'll find another sex partner."

"That's an awesome challenge but I suppose you know that. What are we waiting for? Let's go," I say as I start for the stairs.

"Just a minute, you clean up here, and I'll meet you in my boudoir."

"Boudoir sounds so much sexier than bedroom."

I set a personal best with the cleanup and fly up the stairs. Poor simple me, I am trapped and will probably lose the lottery. Sometimes losing can be so much fun. It's another personal best and it only takes until ten o'clock the next morning. Gineen shakes me awake before leaving for the Casino.

"Poor boy, are you going to sleep all day?" came a familiar voice through the fog.

"Yes, go away. Maybe two days."

"Not on your life. I won the prize and you get out of bed and into the shower right now. I have taken some pity on you and have made your favorite breakfast but if you don't get down here in 15 minutes, I will feed it to the neighbor's dog."

I hate cold showers but this morning it is the only way to disperse some of the fog. I Finish the shower, brush my teeth and climb into fresh jeans and a sweat shirt.

"Did I make the deadline?"

"You actually missed it by five minutes, but I am ready to grant you special dispensation. Provided, of course, that you are ready to go in fifteen minutes."

"Huh. Ready to go where. Hell, I'm ready to go back to bed."

"Don't even think it. We are going for a 10-mile bike ride and then a hike up our favorite trail at Mount Misery. Hurry up, your hash is getting cold. I'm going to be a bit late for work this morning and I'll make it up by working late."

Clearly, I would get nowhere by denying her the thrill of sticking it to me. I eat quickly and then hurry out of the condo with my bike, following Gineen all the way. I mean all the way for her 10-mile ride which ended at the base of Mount Misery.

"Why don't you go on ahead and I will catch up before you reach the top?"

My God, the woman is serious. "Hey, isn't Roger coming by

after work tonight? Maybe we should go home now and get ready for him."

"If you don't shut up and start climbing I may have to tell everyone what a miserable excuse for a man you are. Maybe even get you fired from this job so I can get it done by myself."

I ignore this threat because she probably could get it done by herself.

Well, climb we do, and I must admit I start to feel better by the time we get to the top. But I don't say that out loud for fear she will start on another round of exercises.

CHAPTER IX

"It's six thirty, Roger should have been here a long time ago. I wonder if everything is ok?"

"Stop sounding like a little old man. He'll be here when he's here."

"A startling concept. Have you been working on it a long time?"

"Ouch!" She lands one of her best left hooks to my midsection. Knocks the wind out of me. Luckily, I don't lose my dinner.

"Ok Gineen. It's time you stopped using me for your private punching bag. No more. It's not funny and I have black and blue marks all over my body. It's not funny anymore."

"Poor baby...oops there's the doorbell."

"Come on in, Roger."

"Sorry, I'm so late. The Casino was extremely busy. I didn't want to call you from there."

"Have you had dinner? Can I get you something to eat or drink? Tea?"

"Thanks, Gineen, but I did eat a bit before I left. A cold beer sounds good, though."

"Get our guest a Sam Adams, Arnold."

"So, ok." I do as I am ordered, one more time.

"I can tell by the looks on your faces that you have been up to something. Bring me up to date, please."

"Roger, as you know my illness went away a bit early and I spent most of the day at the Casino gathering up some data.

Arnold, at the same time, did some more surveillance on Sam Lightfoot's place, today."

"And?"

"I saw a visitor to the Lightfoot home whose name is Gordon Brown."

"Really. I guess I am not too surprised, but it is good to confirm that your suspicions are correct. Could you tell if he brought anything with him that could have contained money. Like a briefcase or even a paper sack?"

"He had nothing in his hands. When he left, I saw no point to following him, so I came back here."

"And you, young lady, what were you collecting at the Casino? I was too busy with running things and didn't see what you were up to."

"Well, I hope that no one at the Casino saw what I was doing. During lunch hour when Emily was out of her office, I got a list of the people working in the accounting department and their shifts for the next two weeks. I thought it would be better if I got that information instead of you."

"You are correct. We have some work to do. I think it's too late to start any heavy thinking and planning tonight. It would be better if we did that tomorrow at the end of the day. That gives all three of us time to prepare."

"Good idea, Roger. By the way, one of the things that I haven't been able to pick up when I 've been training are the names and shifts of the people who run the show when you are not there."

"I can get you that information easily. I trust these guys implicitly. You don't really believe that any of that crew could be a member of the gang, do you?"

"Roger. I don't know, but you did trust Emily Brown implicitly, right? I say leave no stone unturned. I think from this day forward it would be a good idea if we consider everyone to be a suspect. Don't you.?"

"I admit that would be the best approach. See you tomorrow and thanks for the beer."

CHAPTER X

Gineen goes off to work the next morning for another day of training leaving me with a day free of any required assignments, save for getting ready for our meeting with Roger tonight. After breakfast, I go for a leisurely walk while I think about this situation. I walk by the hospital and down Broadway to the central business district. I am deep in thought most of the way and barely notice the other pedestrians around me. I think that the thefts from the Casino really are not very surprising. Like Dr. Hand said, you will have some of this thievery anywhere there is someone else's money within easy reach. This situation is different, however. Different because it is clearly an organized theft, planned and carried out by a group rather than one individual's momentary surrender to temptation. I start to wonder if all the members of the gang came here at the same time. This question pops into my head while sitting on a bench. Maybe most of them were already employed by the Casino and were recruited by the leaders who arrived with a criminal history like the Browns. This thought leads me to question whether all the members of the gang had come from Casino Niagara.

That might lead to another way to identify more of the gang members. We could talk to Manly Sand at Niagara and get a list of their employees who left the place around the same time as the Browns. I put this idea on my list to discuss with Roger this evening. There is some benefit to sitting on a park bench and thinking as opposed to sitting indoors at a desk, surrounded by computers and other electronic devices. Lost in thought, I am jolted back to reality by a ragged older man who sits down beside me.

"Say, I've hit on some bad times lately and I wonder if you have some change you might be able to share."

I don't like begging and those who do it, so I am about to say no and go back home, but a wave of humanity washes over me and I change my mind.

"I don't have any change, but here is twenty dollars. Use it however you care to."

He seems surprised at first and I think I see tears in his eyes. He recovers quickly enough and stuffs the bill into his pocket.

"You know I haven't always been walking the streets and begging. It's only been a few months. I worked for years at a steady job and got fired for no good reason."

"Tough break. But you don't need to apologize for that. There are lots of tough breaks in this world. What kind of work did you do?"

"Well, I ain't had much education so I done the best I could. Mostly janitorial work. I wished I knew why they up and fired me. I worked for 20 years at the last place. It left me without anything but a few hundred dollars."

"That's a sad story. It isn't often that a company will fire a long-time employee. Was there a drinking problem?"

"No. Never touched a drop and still haven't. Besides it wasn't a company, it was the Indian Casino and they can do anything they want and not be subject to the ordinary rules."

"You mean the Casino Royale?"

"Yup. That's the place. You familiar with it?"

"I am. Listen why don't you give me your name and tell me how to get in touch with you. Maybe there is some way I can help. I know a few people there."

"I doubt there is anything anyone can do, but my name is

Steve Hendrickson. I got kicked out of my apartment. I am staying with my sister Linda. She's a retired librarian who never married. Her house is not far from here. On School Street. Number 1022. I don't know her telephone number. I'll be getting on. Thanks again for the money. You can be sure it will be used for necessities."

"No thanks necessary and here's another twenty to tide you over until I can see if there is anything I can do. You take care."

"Ok. Thank you again. So long and you take her easy. You are a good man."

As he walks away, I detect a slight limp to his gait. I don't know if he could be any help in identifying members of the gang, but stranger things have happened than a janitor being familiar with the internal workings of a gambling casino. Back home, I make a sandwich and open a can of soup. After lunch, I sit down with a fresh pad and a pencil to make a list of discussion items for the meeting with Roger later in the day.

1) My discussion with Steve Hendrickson.

2) Obtain a list of employees who left Casino Niagara about the same time as the Browns. Compare this with a list of new hires at Royale.

3) Look over names and credentials of Roger's 4-5 Assistant Managers.

4) List of names of employees in the accounting department with work shifts.

5) What are the priorities?

6) Is additional surveillance help needed?

After cleaning up the lunch dishes, I head back out for more exercise. I am becoming a real health nut. It is another warm, sunny day so I drive to Mount Misery and climb to the top. It is becoming a piece of cake. I wonder if there is anything more challenging in the area. Mental note to check it out back at the house. Today, I bring along my small, but powerful SONY portable radio. Lying back on our favorite flat rock, I listen to a station playing golden oldies. Before I know it, I am lulled to sleep by the warm sun and sweet music.

The radio switches to news at 5pm and I awake with a start. And with a face starting to show the effects of sun burn. Quickly down the Mount and home. Fortunately, I arrive before Roger or Gineen. I have time to take a quick shower and order Asian food for delivery. The food and Gineen arrive almost at the same time but Roger doesn't get there until 30 minutes later. We all have big appetites and there is little talk of anything while we eat. I finish first and start to clean up the dishes and put the let overs into the fridge. Now, on to the business of the night. When I finish, we move into the office with our notes to go to work.

"Let me begin," I offer. "This may be nothing, but by twist of nature or some dumb good luck, I stumbled upon a character in the park this afternoon. I was resting on a bench near downtown after some exercise and this rather down and out looking fellow came by and sat down, asked if I had any money to spare. My first impulse was to say no because I hate begging, but something inside me said to give the poor fellow some cash. He sat down after thanking me and we started to talk. To make a long story short, this guy used to work at the Casino but was fired outright not very long ago. He was a janitor and may not be much help with anything, but I took his name and address, just in case. They had recently fired him for no apparent reason. He walked with a slight limp and perhaps he just couldn't perform anymore."

"No way. The Tribal Council takes care of every employee and firing someone outright is virtually unheard of. It is not our way. What is his name?"

"Steve Fredrickson. Hard to tell exactly how old he is but I'd guess he's in his fifties or sixties. And he seemed very angry at someone on the Casino staff, but I don't know who."

"Good job. There is something very wrong about his firing and I will investigate it tomorrow, but quietly. In the meantime, why don't you follow up with him and see if you can get any more information. You may tell him that it is likely that we will take care of him unless he committed some very bad crimes against the Casino. We don't arbitrarily fire any employees. We take care of all our employees, even when they get into trouble. You will find that jobs at the Casino are in very high demand because of our experience in this area. Gineen, you might quietly talk to some of the others on our janitorial staff and see what information you might sweet talk out of them. But tread softly."

"I will."

"Roger, another path I thought about taking is contacting Manly Hand at the Niagara Casino for a list of other employees who might have left the Casino around the same time as the Browns."

"Another excellent idea. Go ahead. That might produce some more names to compare with our hiring files. Here are the names and information on my four Assistant Managers that you asked for. Do a preliminary check on them and we will talk about how far to go with them when we meet next. Also, here is the data on the Accounting staff that you asked for. Perhaps some gentle surveillance as a first step."

"Do you think we should get some additional help on the surveillance?"

"Not yet. I realize this is a large work load for you but do the best you can and take as much time as you need. We can put off our next meeting until a time when you have done all this initial work. At this stage, I still want to keep as few people as possible on the job. Let me know through Gineen, when you are ready to talk. Keep up the good work, both of you. I sense we are getting close to a successful completion. Good night. I am off to home."

"Thanks Roger, have a good night."

When he had gone, we head to the bedroom, much too tired from anything but holding each other. Just before dropping off, I ask where home is for Roger.

"Oh, he has an elaborate penthouse suite on the top floor of the Casino. Comes with the job."

"Really. Have you been there?"

"Just once when he needed some paperwork brought up to him. I just had a quick peek, but it seemed quite luxurious."

"Sounds like a good place to have a small intimate wedding."

"Oh, Patrick we are not there yet. Don't push so hard."

CHAPTER XI

Bright and early the next morning, I go to work with renewed vigor. First on my list is to visit with Steve Hendrickson to see what he might be able to tell about the activity at the Casino that got him fired. I luck out when a knock on his door on School Street produces a woman who I assume is his sister.

"Good morning, my name is Arnold Kowalski. Are you Steve's sister Linda by any chance?"

"Indeed, I am. Steve told me about meeting you yesterday in the park. Nice to meet you. I want to thank you for being so kind to Steve. Right now, he could use a lot of that. He is in a very low place. I have never seen him like this in his whole life. Come on in. Can I get you anything?"

"No, I'm fine. May I speak to Steve, if he's in?"

"Oh, he's in alright. He seldom goes out. You caught him yesterday during one of those rare trips out of the house."

"No need to thank me, Linda. The reason he was fired is important to the top staff at the Casino. The General Manager, Roger Jones told me personally that he had no knowledge of Steve's firing and he wanted to know more about it. Roger insisted that the Tribal Council has a long-standing policy of taking good care of the employees even when they are in trouble."

"That's just it, Mr. Kowalski, Steve was not in any kind of trouble. He is the kindest, most gentle of souls and would never, ever do anything illegal or immoral. And he is totally reliable when it comes to work."

"Please call me Arnold, Linda. I sincerely believe what you tell me about Steve is true and I consider myself a good judge of character. Before we go any further, I am going to ask you a favor. Whatever we say or do here today must be kept in the strictest confidence. I don't want anyone to even know that I was here nor that we are going to rectify what we feel was an injustice on the part of the Casino. Can you promise me that? And I mean no one, even the closest friends or relatives."

"If that helps Steve, I can easily promise that. I already trust you and will help you in any way that I can."

"Good. I will ask Steve to give me the same promise when I talk to him. The reason I need this secrecy is quite simple. We are all but certain that some very bad things are going on at the Casino. It's possible that getting Steve off the staff might be related to these goings on. I don't know that for a fact. If it is, I don't want any of the bad guys to know that I am investigating their behavior. A lot of money is involved. Bad people sometimes do crazy things for money. So, the secrecy protects our investigation and may also protect you two from any harm. We are clearly dealing with bad people."

"Now you have me a bit frightened. I will certainly keep my mouth shut."

"Good. Can I talk to him, now?"

"Yes. He's moping around upstairs in his bedroom. I'll get him. Sit down and get comfortable."

A few minutes later she comes back with Steve in tow.

"Hi Steve, good to see you." His face brightens a bit when he saw me waiting.

"I'm going to leave you gentlemen alone, so you can talk. Would either of you care for some coffee or tea?"

"Thanks, but I am fine."

Steve nods as well, and Linda leaves us alone. I explain the need for secrecy about my visit and he has no problem with it.

I repeat my spiel about the possible bad things going on at the Casino and then get to the point of my visit.

"Steve, there is no question in my mind that the Tribal Council will be voting to take good care of you. It won't take them very long. We have already started the ball rolling so you can relax about that."

"Thank you for that. You are a good person."

"Well it's Roger Jones, the general manager you can thank for that. He is very concerned about what went on with you and we are trying to find out the reason it happened at all. The big question I have for you is do you have any idea why they fired you?"

"No, they gave me no explanation at all. One day I was working there and the next day someone had taken my place. I have no idea why. I did nothing wrong, whatsoever. They paid me a week's severance pay and escorted me out the building. I barely had a chance to get my things out of my locker."

"Let me get this straight. When they fired you, they replaced you right away?"

"Well, a few days before I left, my replacement was there training."

"Do you know his name?"

"Yes. His name is Larry Simonetti."

"Thank you. That may be very helpful for us. I have taken up enough of your time. You will be hearing from the Tribal Council shortly. You take care. And once again make sure you don't breathe a word of this conversation until we say it's ok."

"I will. You have my word and thanks again."

All the way back home the name Larry Simonetti is bouncing around in my brain. Obviously, he had to be a plant and a member of the gang. Why else would they get rid of Steve? He knows nothing about the operation of the Casino. There would be no point in sacking Steve other than to get their own guy in there. I begin to see a pattern where the gang is putting their own people into every level on the staff. Now, that really raises the question about the top level of Roger's assistants. It also raises the question of what possible function could someone on Simonetti's level provide. All that I can think of would just to be a lookout of some kind. I hurry back to the house to call Manley Hand in Niagara Falls.

"Good morning. This is Patrick Ingel in Connecticut and I would like to talk to Manley Hand if he is available."

"Good morning. This is Mister Hand's secretary. Mr. Hand is on an important call right now. Can I have him call you back? I don't think it will be very long."

"Sure. No problem."

I give her the number and go to the kitchen for a cup of coffee. By the time, I have brewed one, the phone rings.

"Hi, this is Patrick Ingel."

"Patrick, this is Manly Hand returning your call. How are you?"

"I'm good and we seem to be making progress in our investigation. We're not there yet but I can begin to see the light at the end of the tunnel."

"Good. I hope the information I gave you was some help."

"Manly, it most certainly was a help and I have another favor to ask of you."

"Anything I can do to help get those rascals into prison, just ask. It will be my pleasure to help."

"What I need is simple. I'd like to know the names of all your employees who worked at the Casino about the same time as the Gordons and left about when they did. Any additional information you might be willing to share would be appreciated. I know that this may be a long list and take some of your time, but it could be helpful."

"Of course. I should have seen the significance of that

information myself when you were here. Missed it."

"I did as well. Too focused on the Gordons to think all that clearly."

"I can get the information gathered in a day or so. Shall I snail mail it or fax it?"

"Fax would be better."

"Done. I hope it helps."

"Thanks Hanley."

Lunch time now and I am too lazy to make something. I sneak over to the Harp and Dragon for a roast beef sandwich and a dark beer. When I arrive back at the house, the faxed information is waiting along with another good luck wish from Hanley. He got it together in a little over two hours. Aha, another hunch has probably paid off as there are four names of Casino Niagara employees who left close in time to the Gordons leaving. I am seeing some more progress and to tell you the truth, I am proud of myself. I retrieve the list of Roger's four assistants and began to think about a way to start probing their backgrounds. I don't think long. This is clearly another job for Sally, albeit a much bigger one. I worry it might be difficult for her to get all this information without exposing herself to her bosses. I decide she can take care of herself, so I dial her up.

"Sally Langone."

"Hello, Sally Langone. This is your close friend in Norwich calling."

"Good. This must mean that you have come to your sense and gotten rid of that no-good woman who attached herself to you."

"Sorry to inform you that we are attached closer than ever. Marriage is in the cards. Probably very soon."

"Bummer. You can't blame a girl for trying. And you should know that I think your friend is a very lucky woman. What can

I do for you, Sherlock?"

"Are you still able to help me with my work, sugar?"

"Why wouldn't I?"

"The last time we talked you were having some problems with other staff members, breathing down your back."

"Well they have backed off. I'm good to go. Talk to me."

"I have three persons of interest that I need some license data for. It's a lot of work and due to your internal difficulties, I'm willing to double the usual rate."

"Nah. Try tripling the rate and we will be in business."

"My goodness, you don't love me anymore."

"Yes, I do, but you are almost a married man so I love your money more."

"Deal. Here are the three people I am tracking. By the way, I'm assuming they all live in Connecticut, but they could also live in Rhode Island. Their names are: John Singleton, Larry Worth and Sidney Aronson. I assume this might take you a few days. Right?"

"Under ordinary circumstances that would be the case. For you I may be able to get it done by the end of the day. Overtime charges would apply, however. Consider the data to be a wedding present. The speed of its access is not. I sincerely wish you two the best of everything."

"And how much cash are we talking about?"

"Six hundred dollars."

"Wow. Are you moving to a larger house, or something?"

"Maybe. Will you come visit me if I do?"

"No."

"I thought not. Six hundred."

"Ok already. Get to work. I'm hanging up before the fee skyrockets anymore."

"Bye, Sherlock."

No other work I can think of. Just wait for Sally to produce the data. A good time for a small diversion and some exercise. I throw a couple of peanut and jelly sandwiches together, put the bike into the Caddy and take off. Destination, East Hampton, to relive a boyhood adventure. I push the speed limit a bit and get there in an hour. Near my house there was the beginning of a 5-mile long downhill ride to the Salmon River and a nearby covered bridge. It was a bike ride I made when I was a kid and when my asthmatic lungs permitted. I park the Caddy at the top and take out the bike. When I start down the hill, I am flying downward for five miles with only a short level stretch here and there preventing me from taking off like a plane. The excuse that I used as a kid was to go fishing in the river down at the bottom. I'd take a pole with me and walk a few miles down-river along the bank and occasionally throw the line into the water. Never saw a fish. Going back up the 5-mile grade was hell. Even now with my much better bike, it takes everything I have to ride back up. I make it and head back home. I don't get there until 6 o'clock and Gineen is already home from work.

"Where in the world were you, sugar pie? Having a date with your friend Sally by any chance?"

"Get out. I did talk to her on the phone before I left and hired her to get some more driver license information. Did she leave it with you?"

"No, dear. I guess she doesn't trust me."

"It's not you. I have always told her not to disclose our information to anyone. In fact, she wished both of us a happy married life."

"So, where were you? I called your cell and did not get an answer. Forgot to turn it on again? Some detective."

"Stop picking on me, Gineen. I took part of the afternoon off and drove to East Hampton where I relived a childhood memory. When I was a kid I used to hop on my bike and ride down a humongous hill that was five miles long. At the bottom was the Salmon River where I would pretend to fish. There was also a covered bridge there. Getting back up the hill was hell, but I made it. I plan to sleep well tonight."

"I'm suitably impressed that the old man could do that. Sounds more difficult than Mount Misery. One day I'd like us to visit that place together."

"When this case is over with, I promise to take you there for a picnic by the river. I can't call Sally now cuz her office is closed. I'll do it in the morning. Let's go out to eat."

"Now you are talking my kind of talk. I think your exertions on the bike tell me you need a shower first."

"Good to have an honest friend."

"Just self-protection."

I jump into the shower, first hot, then cold to wake me up. It works. Gineen and I get into the car after I suggest she drive. I am a bit tired. That bike ride was more than I bargained for.

"I'll make you a deal. I'll pay for dinner old lady, if you promise not to talk about business at all."

"You have a deal old man."

The food is great and who could ask for any better company? We both have salads and baked clams with a bit of wine. We chit chat about growing up and family life including our love lives, such as they were. Gineen steers us home. I think I am asleep before I walk through the bedroom door. So much for 5-mile uphill bike rides. I awake refreshed though, and raring to go. At breakfast, I ask Gineen to give Roger a message from me.

"Ask him to give me a call just as soon as you get there. I have a couple of things I want to discuss with him. It will only take a few minutes but it's very important."

"Care to share with me?"

"Sure, partner. First, I want to warn him immediately about

his assistant, John Singleton. He was on Manley Hand's list."

"What? Another member of the gang? Well I could do that. Why waste a telephone call?"

"I know you could, but I also want to talk to him about starting some work on the replacement janitor, Larry Simonetti."

"I'll tell him. See you later master detective."

"Don't forget the master part!"

"Dream on. Give me a smooch, I must be going."

We smooch, and she flies out the door. At ten, the phone rings and it's Roger.

"Morning Patrick. Sorry it took so long to get back to you, but I wanted to find a place outside the Casino to talk. Thanks for identifying Singleton. It's getting to the point where the only two people I trust now are you and Gineen. It might be useful to have a copy of his license for tracking purpose. Can you get one from your source at the DMV?"

"Already ordered. I'll have it soon. Roger, I want to focus in on Larry Simonetti. He's at the bottom end of the pecking order and I think might be the most vulnerable source of information. What do you think?"

"You have been right about everything else so far. Go ahead, I trust your judgement. I'd be crazy if I didn't. I'll call you in a few days after I've had a chance to digest everything you have turned up so far. Then we'll get together and do some planning for the next phase. Take care."

"You too." I hang up and immediately dial Sally at the DMV.

"Good morning, Sally Langone."

"Morning Sally. It's your best customer."

"In more ways than one."

"Got a small and simple job for you."

"Ah, hold on a second. Sorry, one of my bosses just came by with some paperwork. What's up?"

"Please see if you can get me as much information as you can on one Larry Simonetti. I'd be surprised if he lived anywhere but right here in the Norwich area."

"No problem, we aim to please. Should have it by the end of the day."

"The sooner, the better. I'm waiting on that to begin work."

"By lunch time for double the usual."

"Come on Sally, as much work as you get out of me, you should do it for free."

"Stop by my place for dinner tonight and I will do it for nothing."

"Sally. Sally. You begin to sound like a broken record. You know that's not happening, so you might as well drop that line. See if you can get it this morning and I'll pay you whatever you want. Money is no object on this one. Speed is essential."

"You'll have it before lunch, Sherlock."

"And stop calling me Sherlock."

"Well, I wouldn't think you'd want me to call you by your real name on the phone."

"Good point. Just call me X."

"How about XXX? Bye."

An hour later, the phone rings.

"Hello, who's calling please?"

"Is this triple x?"

"Funny. I've got a pen please give me what you have."

"So business-like. You don't love me anymore."

"I'm waiting."

"Ok. Name Larry Simonetti. Age 28. Copy of the license being faxed as we speak. Address, Number 76 Beech Drive, Norwich. Prior License, Massachusetts, resident address there, number 28 Main Court, Plainville. If you need a copy of his Mass license I can get it, but it will take a while."

"Not necessary, sweetie. Great job."

"You're welcome, bye, bye."

Ha. Plainville is the home of Plainridge Park Casino. I'm going out to Mr. Simonetti's home and see what I can see. It's only a few minutes to Beech Drive where I can see it's a very nice home for a janitor. Must be eight or nine rooms with an attached garage and a swimming pool. No vehicles in the driveway. I go up to the door and ring the bell with a prepared story aimed at telling whoever answers that I made a mistake with the address. No Answer. I go around back and peek in the window of the garage door. Nice. Two vintage Mercedes sports cars in minty condition. A 190sl and what looked like a 450sl. Being a janitor at a gambling casino must pay well. I wonder what he drove to work. I have no recent experience with home values and certainly none here in Norwich, so I skip over to the tax assessor's office to see if I can dig out the information on assessed valuation. The assessor is a busty bleached blonde who turns out to be very helpful. My charm, no doubt.

"Good morning. I'm looking for some information on property owned by a gentleman named Larry Simonetti."

"Hello, yourself. Which of his properties are you interested in?"

"To be honest, I didn't know he owned more than one."

"Indeed, he does. According to my records, he owns three residential properties and one commercial. What information would you like on the properties?"

"If it would not be too much trouble, I'd like a list of the four properties with their addresses and assessed valuation."

"Better that that I can simply print out the assessment sheet on each of the properties. Would that suit your purposes?"

"It would."

She put the sheets in an envelope and hands it to me.

"Is there anything else I can do for you?"

"No, thank you very much." (Yeah there is. Brush your frizzy hair and deep six the cheap perfume.)

I drive out to look at the addresses on the valuation sheets. Of the three residential properties, all are of a substantial quality but the home is the most impressive. The commercial property turns out to be a small strip mall with eight small businesses in it including a barber shop, a tobacco shop, a small neighborhood variety shop, an ice cream shop, a watchmaker and three vacant spaces. I snap a few photographs of the mall, as I had with the residential properties. The valuation for all the properties adds up to close to three million dollars. I guess this was probably on the conservative side. Nice bunch of real estate for a janitor. I'd love to see the balances in his checking and savings accounts but that's too difficult a job for me to pull off. At least just now. Besides, I really don't need it. I am certain I am looking at a key figure in our case. I go back to Simonetti's house and just as I get there, he drives into the driveway. Another Mercedes! A new small sedan. His everyday car, I guess. No point messing around there anymore so I go on home. In the office I put together a dossier on our prosperous janitor. Gineen walks in as I am putting the last few notes and photographs into place.

"What are you working on? Doesn't look like you were doing any hiking or cycling today."

"No ma'am. Look at these photos."

"Yeah, so. What am I looking at?"

"You, dear woman, are looking at about 3-4 million dollars of real estate owned by the most prosperous janitor in the world."

"I don't get it. Who or what are we talking about?"

"Why Larry Simonetti, of course."

"You're kidding. Right? Jesus, you've done it again. You are proving to be a very good P.I. I might even hire you the next time I need a divorce."

"I don't think so because it's me you will be married to and I refuse to let you go. How about a hug?"

"Aw shucks, you can have a hug and a kiss too. But that's all. No sex tonight."

"Dinner and a movie then?"

"Good. How about *Casablanca*? There at least 20 or 30 lines of dialogue that I haven't memorized."

"Play it again, Sam."

We both love that movie. Watching it together is great fun for both of us. We watch it in the living room on the big screen and nibble on left-over pizza. A nice evening to top off a very productive day. As we hold each other just before fading into sleep, I say to her, "I don't mind admitting to you that I am a bit proud of myself for the work I did today."

"Long way to go but I do think Roger will be pleased. Good night love-man."

Just before I turn on the outside lights that cover the grounds, I glance out the window and spot two people sitting in a car in front on the house. Strange. I wonder if they are Roger's security guards sent to watch over us. I call him immediately and tell him about the guys in a car.

"Are they your security guards, Roger?"

"Is there any place you can go to sneak out of the house, without them seeing you?"

"No there isn't."

"I don't like the sound of this. I will send two guards out there as soon as I hang up. It'll take them about ten minutes to get there. In the meantime, you do whatever is necessary to protect the two of you. My guys will clean up whatever mess is there."

"OK"

"Gineen, quickly lock yourself into the back bedroom. There may be some trouble heading this way."

"What kind of trouble?"

"Dammit woman do what I tell you, NOW"

She gets the message and runs to the back bedroom and I hear the click of the lock and the security chain being put into place.

I go back to the window and see two people getting out of the car and heading for the front of the house. I grab my gun and run to the front door flinging it open and surprising the two who are carrying pistols pointed at the ground. The best defense is an active offense. I recognize them as the two brothers that I shot back in New Haven. I blast through the door taking them by surprise. I raise my gun and point it at the guy on the left since he is closer to me. Instead of stopping he starts to raise his gun.

My military training kicks in and **BAM.** I drop him with a shot to the center of body mass. Oh God, I have killed him. I start to feel sick to my stomach. Then I remember the second brother and swing around toward him. He's turned his back to me, running back to the car. I just can't shoot a man in the back. He jumps into the car and takes off like a bat out of hell.

I stand there, shivering over the body and know that I have killed a man. It seems like hours but it is probably only a couple of minutes until Roger's two security men pull up. At the same time Gineen comes flying out the front door, screaming, "Patrick, Patrick."

One of the newly arrived guards grabs my gun and orders us to get in the house. We comply without a peep to let them clean up the mess.

For a while I can't stop shivering. I hold Gineen and lean on her for support. Outside there is a sea of flashing blue lights which are quickly turned off at the behest of Roger's guards. I am still cold and trembling for another hour.

"It's ok Patrick. You had no choice. It was him or you and

you made the right choice. You saved my hide in the process."

It takes a while, but I finally calm down. We are getting near a solution to the Casino's problem. I realize that it won't be solved without me having all my wits about me. With Gineen's help, I fall asleep after a few hours and sleep restlessly the rest of the night.

During breakfast, I remember I wanted to talk to Roger. I decide to ask him if he could come by this evening. Faced with another day with nothing specific to do, I drive up to Plainville to see if I can find out anything more about Larry Simonetti. First, I go on a short but fast bike ride to get the blood flow and maintain the daily exercise routine that I'm developing. I'll do some more when I got back. The drive to Plainville is about 63 miles. It takes me about an hour and a half, so it is late morning when I arrive at the casino. I eat lunch at one of their restaurants and then go to the manager's office. I tell his secretary that I was a P.I. doing a background investigation on one of their former employees.

"Well", says she, "let me show you where our personnel office is. I'm sure they can help you."

"I'd much prefer to talk to the manager, if he is available."

"He is busy right now, and I can't get you in to see him for about an hour."

"Ok. I'll take a walk around the casino and come back in 45 minutes."

I gather she is peeved at me for not taking her advice to see the personnel department. Just protecting her boss. I suppose. Their casino is a nice place but after I've walked around for a short while I decided that if you have seen one, you have seen them all. So, I kill a little time with a Sam Adams beer. Like they say, it is cocktail time somewhere in the world. Back to the secretary, who keeps me waiting the requisite 15 minutes and then shows me into the manager's office.

"Good afternoon, Mark Adams. My secretary tells me you are investigating one of our former employees."

"Yes. Good to meet you. My name is Arnold Kowalski. I am a private investigator in Connecticut and I am indeed checking into the work history of one of your ex- employees whose name is Larry Simonetti. My client in Connecticut has some suspicions about him. We know his last job was in your casino and he has shown up recently down there at our place. Can you tell me anything about his work here?"

"My secretary has gotten his work history from the personnel department. He was a janitor here and I have no recollection of him myself. According to the records he quit recently. He indicated to his boss that he was returning to his home territory and we have not heard from him since."

"Did he have a clean record while he was here? Fights with other employees, failure to take orders or do his job well. Anything unusual?"

"No, nothing in the file like that."

"Missing funds?"

"Certainly not. He had a very good job performance record here and we wouldn't hesitate to give him a good recommendation, but so far nobody had asked for one. Are there any other questions I might be able to answer?"

"No. I can't think of anything."

"Please understand, everything I told you came from the personnel department, because as I told you, I don't believe I've ever met the gentleman. The personnel director is tip top and I trust her implicitly."

"Well, thanks for your time. Oh, by the way, have you experienced any incidents of missing cash recently?"

"So, that's is what this is all about. Let me tell you something, Arnold. Any casino or other business that handles as much cash as we do finds itself with problems having to do with theft. We have had our share, but they have all been small ones. We caught the perpetrators in every case. Simonetti was not involved in any of them."

"Ok. Thanks for your time. You have been very helpful."

"Glad to be of help. Good bye."

"So long."

While I am driving back home, I turn over in my mind exactly what I learned from that interview. It is clear the staff at Plainville trusted Simonetti, but I know that Roger would agree with me that implicit trust may not be so trustworthy. I suppose Adams might have had some substantial losses and not want to divulge them. I discount that theory. Human nature says that people want a chance to get their money back or see the thief punished. I guess it would be fair to say I didn't learn anything at all on this trip. Can't win them all. Back home before Gineen. I have enough time for another vigorous bike ride after the inactivity on the drive. She still is not back after the ride, so I decide to surprise her with dinner. Sweet and sour cabbage soup and grilled salmon. She gets in late enough that I am almost through getting ready. The table is set with candle light along with a cooling bottle of champagne.

She walks in the door at seven and exclaims, "Oh, my God how did you know? This is just what I need after a grueling day."

She rushes at me and jumps up with her arms and legs wrapped around me, nearly knocking me over.

"Champagne and candlelight. Perfect. Do I have time for a shower?"

"You do if you hurry."

She is back down in fifteen minutes, dressed in a tee shirt and shorts with her wet hair pulled back in a pony-tail. She is beautiful in anything she wears. Or doesn't wear.

"What a day at the Casino. Millions of gamblers all over the place and we had to do end of the month records preparation. Roger said to tell you that he will not be here tonight. Tomorrow at six. What about your day?"

"I drove up to the casino in Plainville, Massachusetts to see if I could find out any information about our rich janitor."

"You mean Simonetti, of course."

"I do. I met with the manager of the place and he insisted that Simonetti had a squeaky-clean record while he worked there. He supposedly left to come down here because this is home to him. He claimed to trust Simonetti implicitly. We know how that goes sometimes. Don't we?"

"I guess we do indeed."

"He did say that they had an occasional theft problem, but they were all small and the thieves were found and were no longer working at the casino."

"So, what do make out that information?"

"Honestly, I'm not sure. It's possible he did leave there to come home. That's a question for more research. But it's also possible he saw the Royale as a bigger and better opportunity. Who knows? He might have been recruited by the gang. Perhaps you can find out what shifts he is working in the next week or so and maybe we can keep our eyes on him. I'm going to do the dishes. Why don't you look for a movie?"

"I'm not in a movie mood, Sherlock. *I'm in the mood for love. Simply because you're near me...oh, oh,* oh, *oh, I'm in the mood for love.*"

"Keep practicing and one day you will make Barbara Streisand's version of the song sound pale by comparison. In the meantime, don't give up the day job." I dodge a left jab. Something I'm getting better at with all the practice.

I do the dishes and she drags some pillows and a blanket into the living room. I join her after making a fire in the fireplace and we make beautiful music together.

I awake at nine to the smell of coffee.

"You're up already?"

"What do you mean already? It's nine o'clock and I'm off to work. I left you some coffee in the kitchen. Ta. Ta."

I take a long shower to wake up. I feel good but still thinking about our rich janitor a lot as I dress and eat breakfast. I can't see any way to do anymore work on him. I switch my focus to our alleged co-conspirator, one Assistant Director John Singleton. Since I am going to be nosing around town, I put on one of my mild disguises. Jeans, a funky tee shirt, sunglasses and a Patriots cap. At the local Enterprise Rental Agency, I rent a small economy car for the day. I already have Singleton's address.

He doesn't live in Norwich but south in Mystic Seaport. This is a wealthy town on Long Island Sound. Even the older, smaller homes are lovely. Singleton's home is directly on the water in a big old mansion that is partially obscured by a wall and iron gate. I manage to park across the street where I have a limited view of the front of the mansion. There is a Rolls Royce or Bentley parked out front. I'm not close enough to see the hood ornament so I can't tell which one it is. There is a man fussing over the car who appears to be either Singleton or a chauffeur. Just then an elegantly dressed woman comes out of the front door, stops to pick a rose off one of the many bushes and then jumps into the back seat of the car while the gentleman holds the door. Chauffeur!

No point to follow them as they head south on Interstate 95. Probably a shopping trip to New York. Instead I go to the local tax assessor's office to get a valuation report for the mansion. Mansions this big usually have a name, but I didn't know if this one did. I take the report out to the car where I look it over. The property consists of the parcel that the house was on as well as a large vacant lot on both sides. The rich like privacy. My god the assessed valuation is 16 million dollars. Crime seems to be paying very well. This place makes the janitor's place look like, well, a janitor's place. Back to the mansion, where I stick my camera through the iron bars of the gate for a few quick photos to give to Roger. Suddenly, a large dog of unknown lineage comes charging toward the gate. I think for a moment he will crash right through it. He pulls up inches from the gate and proceeds to bare his fangs and snarl. I am not afraid, but nevertheless ferl it wise to get out of there as quick as I can. Well, maybe a little afraid. I jump into my Chevrolet economy car which is half the size of the dog and floor it. Maybe a lot afraid. I don't like dogs and they don't like me.

I keep a lookout via the rear-view mirror, half expecting to see that giant animal loping after me and knocking me off the road into a ditch. I drive back home safely and return the rental car unscathed to Enterprise. I'm making fun, but I really didn't like to think what that dog would have done had I been inside the gate. Instead of going to the house, I hop over to Mount Misery, climb to the top and sun myself for a half an hour before I return home to an empty house. I am certainly not in the mood to make dinner for the three of us, so I order Asian food to be delivered at six. My timing turns out to be perfect. Gineen arrives at 5:45 and Roger minutes later.

"Mr. Detective, I don't see a delicious dinner on the stove? Do I? Y'know Roger is right behind me it would be good to have something waiting for the man that feeds you. Tell me where I am wrong, to coin a phrase."

"And how was your day Ms. Management trainee? You are wrong from start to finish. Things are not always what they seem on first look. In fifteen minutes or so, there will be a knock on the door and a feast fit for kings will arrive on schedule. All arranged and paid for by a lowly soldier working in the trenches. What do you say to that?"

"How clever of you. That might earn you a small hug and kiss."

"Very nice. Do you..."

"No, I don't think we have time for a quickie. Roger is right behind me."

Right on schedule, a knock on the door which I open for Roger.

"Good evening, boss. Come on in. I have a grand dinner almost on the table and a beautiful and charming hostess to help serve it."

"Are you ok, Patrick?"

"Why, I am better then ok. I am super. Comes from a hard day of detecting out there in the real world."

I don't have time to explain before there is another knock on the door. When I open it this time in walks a young delivery man carrying bags of aromatic Asian food. We set that feast down on the table and I after I pay him for it along with an extra generous tip he leaves. A few minutes later the three of us sit down to eat.

"Don't look now Roger, but my friend has been acting strange. I may have to send him to his room if he doesn't shed that shit eating look off his face. Pardon my language."

"Now that you mention it, he does look like the cat who swallowed a canary."

"Hey, you two can stop having fun at my expense. After all, I had a busy and productive day on the job."

"I can see that you can hardly wait to tell us just exactly you produced today, so out with it."

"I hope some of what I saw today will be some help and I think it will be. First, I drove up to Plainville, Massachusetts and talked to the manager of the casino. He thought that our rich janitor, Simonetti, did a fine job up there. He insisted that he left voluntarily for a job back in his old home town. According to him the casino has not suffered any large thefts, but he left the door open a tiny crack. To quote him, in so many words, any business that handles a large amount of cash will have thefts. He claimed that any they have had have been solved and he did not believe Simonetti was involved in any of them. Still, I keep asking myself how a janitor accumulates 3-5 million dollars' worth of real estate. Further, with that asset base why go looking for another janitor's job? I believe he is still a strong suspect. And then we come to your Assistant Manager John Singleton. I drove down to Mystic Seaport to see what I might find out about your trusted assistant. He lives directly on the water in a very elaborate home which I can only describe as a mansion. I made a trip to the tax assessor's office where I learned that it is assessed at 16 million bucks. It is protected by a high wall with an iron gate. I watched for a while and a tall, slender, and very beautiful woman came out of the house and got into a chauffeur-driven Rolls Royce. I couldn't get a good look at her but by the way she carried herself, I'm guessing she was somewhat younger than 30. The limo got on the highway and headed west in the general direction of New York. You must pay very good wages at the Casino or maybe he inherited his wealth. If that is the case, it's a bit strange that he is working in your Casino."

"He is paid well, but of course not well enough to afford a 16 million-dollar home. From top to bottom the Casino is loaded with suspicious employees, who are stealing us blind. Patrick, I am not sure exactly how to proceed but it must be in such a way that one of them gives up the other members of the gang. I wonder if I should bring in the other members of the Tribal Council and ask for advice?"

"Roger, I don't see what the other members of the Council could add to your own resources. Besides you have been living with the problem for some time and know most, or all, of the people involved. We just need to put our collective heads together and develop a foolproof plan to capture the gang in the act of looting the Casino. Maybe it takes us a while to find the correct path. My guts tell me we can do it. I know we can. The three of us bring plenty of smarts to the table. It's your decision, of course"

"I think Patrick is right," Gineen chimes in. "And if he isn't and we fail, you could always bring the rest of the Council members in at any time. Couldn't you? I think we should wait before we bring any other Council members in."

"I guess you are both right. I'm just running low on confidence that we can get the job done. And I am worried that the longer this looting goes on, the shakier our financial condition becomes. Meanwhile, the gang accumulates tons of money and with it, power. Much power. After all, money is power. I am starting to lose faith that we will be able to stop them cold."

"Perhaps we each need to back off a little bit from the problem and do some more thinking about the solution. If we do it independent of each other and then meet to put a plan together we just might find the right answer," says Gineen.

"That makes good sense to me. You see it's not just your beauty that drew me to you, it's your intelligence and good judgement," I add.

"You liar. We all know what you were after. Just shut up or I'll have to whack you in the stomach or some other place where it would hurt even more," she says with a giggle. This bit of humor is enough to lift some of the tension from the room. I am surprised that she would talk like this in front of Roger but the smile on his face tells me he is ok with it.

"Why don't we take two days to mull it over and then get back together?"

We agree to that idea and finish our meal at a leisurely pace which, I think, reflects a certain amount of relief for each of us.

"Next time Roger, the food is on you. Something different would be good."

"I'll see what I can do. Time for me to go. You two have a good evening."

"Good night, Roger."

When he is gone, I put my arms around Gineen and say, "You know I was serious when I said it was more than your beauty that attracted me to you."

"That's good because the beauty is now too busy thinking about this mess to play house with you."

"Bummer. I know. I can feel the wheels going around and round in your head. The noise level of all those gears is deafening."

I go up to the bedroom leaving her sitting in an office chair with a distant look in her eyes. In the morning, we have breakfast together, but she still does not want to talk about putting a plan together. She is out there somewhere and short of a life-threatening emergency she can't be reached.

"Patrick, it will be better if we each develop an idea separately so that when we get together tomorrow, we will have three independently developed ideas. I'm going to work, now. I'll see you at dinner."

"Sure. You have a good day."

Now what do I do? We have never spent such a distant time together. I sense she is taking the thefts personally as though, somehow, she is responsible. Oh well, she is a big girl and will work it out. Faced with whole day in front of me I go back to exercising my body. Maybe some of that will rub off on my mind. Out to Mount Misery where I punish myself with a full tilt run up to the top, without stopping. At the top, there is someone sunning herself on my favorite flat rock. She is young and quite beautiful. I am huffing and puffing, bent over with my hands on my hips.

"Practicing for the Boston Marathon, by any chance?" she asks with a smile.

"No. Just trying to clear my head."

"There must be a better way than that. Hi, I'm Silvia."

"Arnold."

"Is this the place where I say, Come here often?"

"No, I think that might be a little too corny."

"I've been here for an hour and this rock is starting to feel like a rock so I'm going back down. Care to join me for coffee and donuts?"

"Thanks for the invitation but I just got here. I have some serious thinking to do. Maybe another time."

"Ok. Perhaps another time. You take care."

"You too," say I as she turns and takes off down the trail.

Now that she is standing and walking away, I think to myself what a spectacular looking woman, even from the back. The old Patrick would surely have accepted her invitation. How times have changed. I ease myself down on the rock with my back up against a tree, close my eyes and let the sun's rays work me over.

I am awfully close to falling asleep when my mind clicks into low gear and I start to think about the problem at hand. I throw a bunch of wild assed ideas away and suddenly realize there is only one way we were going close the case. We have to catch someone in the act of stealing our cash, of course. To do that, we need to find out who is physically taking it, how they are getting it into their pockets. Catch them Right in the act. I realize that I don't know diddly squat about the process by which the cash moves from the accounting department to the bank. I need to know more about that before I will get anywhere. All I really know is the money is taken to the bank via an armored car service. I don't even know which one it is, or which bank they deliver it to. I know virtually nothing about that chain of events. I will ask Roger to define that chain when we meet. Clearly the money is not being stolen directly from the gaming areas. Just too hard to do right out in front the mass of security people and customers. My bet is that the assistant manager must know all the details concerning the thefts. And he would know every single one of the gang members. I could not learn anything about his routine from the outside. This would have to come from Roger of Gineen. I can do the outside surveillance and documentation once we learned the details of how the money is getting out of the Casino.

Now, I could use that coffee and donuts. Down the trail at a leisurely pace and I do stop for a snack. There is not much I could do for the rest of the day today. I go out for lunch at a nearby Burger King and then get on the bike. I ride up to Mohegan Park, a beautiful, well-kept facility with rose gardens and water where you can fish. I ride all around the park and pick a place where I can throw a blanket down on the ground and rest. As relaxed as I am, I still can't get the Casino completely out of my thoughts. I start to make a mental list of the possible things that I can do to fill up the day tomorrow and advance the cause. Maybe I would visit the homes of Simonetti and Singleton in the hope of spotting someone from the Casino. Perhaps put on a little disguise and see what I could learn about how the money moves from the cashier's area to the armored cars and then to the bank. Is it possible any of the armored car drivers are members of the gang? I make another mental note to raise this question tomorrow with Roger. I could fill up the day with some or all these activities, so I finally give myself the rest of the afternoon off and quickly fall asleep on the ground. I look at my watch when I am rudely awakened by a herd of young kids being young kids. My thoughts automatically go to Gineen. Will we ever get married and have children? At age 39 isn't time running out for me? Maybe not, older guys than I have started families. Is this me thinking about a mundane married life?

I bike back home and am just getting off the bike when Gineen drives up. We hug, and she whispers in my ear, "I apologize for being so distant last night and this morning, but you know I get like that sometimes."

"Well no, I have never seen that before, at least for that long a time. Welcome back. But I understand. You are back. Yes?"

"I am. Did you really miss me or are you just trying to make me feel good?"

"Get out of here. Of course, I did."

"Where have you been?"

"I've been physical again today. You have really started something with this exercise stuff. A top speed run up Mount Misery and then I biked around Mohegan Park."

"I hope you saved some of your energy for me. I was counting on a workout to make up for last night."

"You can count on it. You want to start right now or wait til after dinner?"

"Um, can't we do both?"

"You're on. Should we start right here on the street or go inside?"

"Get inside man funny man and get out of those sweaty clothes."

"Yes commander. Any other orders, ma'am?"

"Yes. Take a shower and be ready for me."

"I have to tell you that I am ready now."

"Stop babbling and go, already."

I go. We have a great evening that stretches late into night. Starting with a walk around the neighborhood. And then dinner and later on a movie.

"Gineen. It was so refreshing to meet people a few feet away who have nothing to do with casinos and theft problems."

She makes dinner and I pick the movie, *Night of the Hunter* with Robert Mitchum and Shelley Winters. The absolute best night I have ever had in my entire life. In the morning, Gineen goes to work early. I decide to do some snooping around the place where the money is picked up by the armored car service. A bit of a disguise in order again so I put on a Red Sox ball cap and pull it down on my forehead. Sun glasses. I put on a pair of ragged jeans and that is the extent of it. Probably enough for me to blend in the crowd and might get me by some of the people who know me. In any event, I am not going inside so I am safe. I rent a small economy car from Enterprise again and drive to a parking space near the rear loading dock of the Casino, the location where the money is loaded into the armored cars. I am in luck. About thirty minutes later one of the cars pull up. Luck never hurts. I wander over to the area and watch the brief transfer of funds, packaged in two large bags equipped with locks. The money is taken out onto the loading dock by two Casino employees who I do not recognize. The transfer to the two armored car guards takes just a couple of minutes. They sign several forms and leave. I am too far away to see any details on the forms. The third guard, the driver of the car, stays in his seat the entire time. One of the guards lifts the money bags into the rear of the car while the other one watches his back, armed with a small shotgun, or automatic short barreled rifle. I can't tell which, and I wouldn't want to be looking at the front end of either one. Both guards have stern, serious looks on their faces and there is no doubt in my mind they would use the weapons with provocation. I sense that they are starting to get curious about me, so I walk casually back to my car as they enter the rear of their vehicle. When they take off, I follow several cars behind them. When they get to the bank, the bags are unloaded, and I take off.

I don't know what I was hoping to learn on this escapade, but I now know a few details about the transfer from the Casino and maybe that will turn out to be helpful. Wishful thinking, probably. There are lots of dead ends in the detective business so one gets used to them and automatically turns to the next lead to follow. I can't think of any other many potential leads on this part of the cash transfer process to follow but there are others to follow. First, I drive to the home of our rich janitor, Simonetti, to check it out again. It is quiet there with nothing obvious happening. What the hell, I decide to knock on the door to see what will happen. I grabbed my ever-present clipboard. I ring the bell and the door opens. Standing in it is a little gray-haired lady, who looks me over carefully before she undoes the chain lock. My honest face at work.

"What can I help you with young man?"

"Good morning. My name is Hubbard and I am doing a survey for the power company. Is Mr. Simonetti at home?"

"Why no, he is working. Are there any questions that I can answer? I am his mother."

"No ma'am. I can only speak to the person listed on my form. I'll try another time. Thank you so much and I hope I didn't disturb you. Bye now."

Next up I drive down to Mystic Seaport to check out Singleton's place once more. I told you detective work is often very boring. The mansion is every bit as imposing to me as it was the first time. I park across the street where I can see a portion of the mansion through the gate. All quiet. No dogs visible. I wait patiently for an hour and a half. I half expect the police to come by and check me out. Or maybe a private security guard. I need to pee and as I am turning the key to start the engine, Singleton's Rolls pulls up to the front door of the mansion, the chauffeur gets out and opens the rear door. A man gets out and it is clearly Singleton. Then another man with a suitcase who I have no possibility of identifying follows. I think the suitcase guy might be staying overnight, but both Singleton and he come out of the mansion about 15 minutes later and head north. Back to the Casino, I guess. Damn. If I can beat them back to the Casino I might have a chance to ID suitcase guy, maybe even snap a picture for Roger.

No way am I going to beat them back with my little economy box. Sure enough, by the time I get back, there is no sign of the Rolls nor any of its occupants. I just know that suitcase was packed with Casino cash and I blew a chance to bust the case wide open. Maybe we could learn something about suitcase guy from the Casino records. Assuming, of course, that he is a Casino employee. I return my rental car and go back home to wait for Gineen and Roger. They arrive just after six, right on schedule. Both carrying large bags of take out food.

"How nice to see you both and the food, too. Come on in. I am starved."

"Well, nice to see you too. We are here, next to the food in case you missed us. How unusual for you to be hungry. Do I at least get a hug?" She gets one.

We take the food into the dining room. I am eager to eat. I can't help it. While they are washing up, I hurriedly set the table and get the food out of the bags with lightning speed. Wow. Roger really brought a spectacular meal. I manage to sample a bit before they even get to the table.

"Roger, you did it right. Take it from me, an expert on food."

"You mean an expert on eating don't you, loveman? You'll have to excuse him Roger, there is nothing on Earth more important to him than eating. Ever since his mommy told him to clean his plate because there were children everywhere who were starving. You might think he has never seen a chicken before. Relax sweetheart and let me pour us some wine to start with. I know you'd prefer beer but it's hard to make a toast with a beer bottle. Here's to a successful solution to the Casino's problem."

"Yea. I'll drink to that," says Roger. "And another toast to a happy couple who are right here with me."

"And so will I," I add. "I believe I came within a whisker of blowing this case wide open today."

Glasses stopped in midair!

"Really. And how did that happen, Sherlock?"

"Like this, Ms. Boss. After you left for work this morning, I decided to do a bit more surveillance to see if I could learn anything at all that might give us a clue to the identity of more of our gang members. I rented a small car and used some sunglasses and a baseball cap as a disguise. I had no intention of going into the Casino itself, but I wanted to take another look at the back-door cash transfer operation. I parked near the rear loading platform and watched the armored car personnel pick up the morning's take from the Casino. I did this because I was wondering if the guards could be accomplices. I learned nothing. Roger, do you think there is any possibility of this happening?"

"I doubt it very much, but I have been wrong so many times lately. So just put that idea on a back burner until we can figure out a way to check it out. Don't forget, we do not want to alert anyone that we are on to the gang, particularly if they are involved. It could blow our entire investigation."

"I can't believe the armored car guys are involved. Next, I drove over to our wealthy janitor's house intending to do a bit of surveillance. His car was not there so I took a chance and knocked on his door, assuming he was at work. I have a phony story ready about a reported power outage. A gray-haired older lady opened the door and once she sees the clipboard in my hand she is eager to talk and talk she did. She is Simonetti's mother. I didn't see any point to talking extensively with her if he is involved. It could tip him off. I thanked her and left. So far, pretty much a lost day. Lots of lost days in detective work. One last bit of the trail was Singleton's mansion in Mystic Seaport, so I drive there. This is the place where I come close to making some major inroads into the case. I watch the mansion from across the street and in comes Singleton's Rolls. I see two men get out of the car. One who I could not identify is carrying a small suitcase and the other is Singleton. I assume that suitcase guy is a visitor who will be staying overnight. Not so. They both came out a few minutes later, get in the car and drive off north toward the Casino. I just know that suitcase was full of your cash, Roger. But hell, I don't have any way to prove it."

"You couldn't identify suitcase guy? Is there anything about him that might be helpful if you saw him again?"

"Hard to say because I only saw him for a few seconds. Wait a minute. Now that you ask, I believe he had a slight limp. I'm not completely sure of that so if he did limp, it must have been a very minor one."

"Patrick, you may have given us a clue that will push us over the brink. I don't recall anyone at the Casino who limps but if it is very slight I could easily have missed it. What about you Gineen?"

"Nobody comes to mind. We should keep a lookout in the Casino. Perhaps we can ID him through the limp."

"Ok. The two of us need to go back to the Casino to check out all the employees in the cashier's office and look for a limp. Maybe we get lucky. I hope we get lucky. If we don't, we will deal with that later. I have a good feeling about this lead. Patrick, as always you are doing a magnificent job and I look forward to dropping a very large reward in your lap as I promised."

"Nonsense, Roger. All he wants is a lot of food to eat. Perhaps you can buy him a supermarket."

"I think a sense of humor is good for the soul even during trying times, like these, but must I always bear the brunt of the humor?"

"More than anything else, I am looking forward to hosting your wedding. Let's get back to work and solve this case so we can unite you two forever."

"Hey, I have already asked her several times and each time she turned me down. She wasn't ready or some such nonsense. Perhaps if you put in a good word, it might help."

"For goodness sake will you two so-called gentlemen stop talking about me as if I wasn't here! Roger if you drop a bundle of cash in his lap, he **REALLY** will be impossible to live with."

"Perhaps, I will drop half a bundle in his lap and half in yours. Does that work?"

"Oh yeah, a lot better. It's decided then."

"Now who's talking like I wasn't here? Maybe I ask Simonetti's mother to marry me. Maybe he will give us a shopping center."

"You'd go well with a gray haired old lady. So, it's decided. Now shut up and eat."

"Always the boss."

"Correct."

"And always the last word."

"Correct."

"Alright children, now that we have your personal relationship squared away, I'm going home. After we check out our employees for one with a limp, Gineen will let you know what we find. Then we'll get together once more to plot strategy. I'll tell you right now that I have a good feeling. It shouldn't take long, a day or two to cover all the shifts. Til then behave and stay out of trouble. Good night."

"Roger before you go make a note to check the time sheets for today and find out who was not working at the time I saw suitcase man."

"I know that Stapleton was working. I will check the personnel records to find out who was not working. Another good idea. Good night again and thanks for dinner. It was productive and pleasant at the same time. Now you two go and plan your wedding. It will be in my suite at the Royale if you want. I hope you will do. It will be a Royal wedding. I can promise you that."

"Goodnight, Roger," we chirp together.

When he has left Gineen and I sit staring at each other for a few moments. Finally, she raises her arms, palms up. "Why not?" she says with a giggle and a mischievous look on her face. We stand, and she runs at me and jumps on me with both legs wrapped around my hips, almost knocking me over.

"Let's go to bed and make mad passionate love all night long."

"Oh no, not yet. One thing is missing. It's called a proposal."

"Oh, come on, Gineen, it doesn't work like that anymore."

"It does for me. I'm old fashioned. Down on your knee." Another order.

Down on one knee I take her outstretched hand.

"Will you marry me? "

"I'll think about it. Now get up the stairs and get ready for me to ravage you, while I clean up the dishes."

A fair swap I think to myself. I don't dare voice it for fear of getting the dishwasher's job. It turns out to be a fair fight. We take turns ravaging each other.

"I call it a draw. I want a rematch at your earliest possible convenience."

"Hah. That will be in about a week. Turn the lights out I am going to work in the morning and it is already 1 am."

I mumble a few last love words in her ear and then turn the lights off.

In the morning, I again find myself with no specific assignments for the day. I go back over the past few days in my mind as I munch my rice sugar frosted flakes. It is now too late to check out the morning cash pickup at the Casino, so I drive to Simonetti's house, where I sit and watch for two hours. I don't get to use the camera that I have brought along. No point to bugging the old lady again. Next stop on my routine which is getting just a bit boring is the mansion. Another couple of hours drag by without anything at all happening. What the hell, I leave and drag out the bike for a ride to Mt. Misery which is beginning to feel like my home away from home. I chain the bike to a tree at the base and then jog to the top. I am getting proficient at this exercise shit. As I reach the summit the sky clouds up and soon it is raining. Well not raining, pouring. God bless New England weather. I walk carefully down the slope to the bike and then pedal through the streets which have developed puddles deep enough to hide a Volkswagen. Just my luck, Gineen is home early, just in time to catch me dog paddling into the house. As usual, she takes no pity on me and starts to giggle.

"When did you start swimming with your clothes on? You look dreadful."

"That's because I feel dreadful. I am in no condition for any of your dreadful humor, either."

"Aw, poor boy, you are absolutely right. I apologize."

"You do? There is a first time for everything, isn't there?"

"Since I might marry you, I thought I should be developing my house frau side. Take off your clothes and I will wash them for you."

"So nice of you, delivered with a note of sarcasm. You just want to get me naked. Admit it."

"Well there is that. But go take a shower while I make you a nice dinner."

I shower and dress in some warm clothes and go back downstairs where I find dinner on the table (last night's left overs) and candle light.

She throws her arms around me and says, "Come eat your dinner before it gets cold. I've saved the best surprise for last, as if you don't know what that is."

I pretend not to know what she is talking about. "Apple pie and Haagen Daz?"

"I'll show you after Roger leaves."

"Roger's coming over tonight?"

"Oh yeah. I forgot to tell you, he will be here at seven thirty."

"I'll do the dishes while you go freshen up."

"Oh, you think I need freshening up?"

"Sometimes your best fiends won't tell you."

She comes back into the room just as I am letting Roger in.

"I am sorry that I'm so late. I hope I am not interrupting anything."

"Well Roger, you are. Gineen and I were just about to practice making a baby."

"Oh, shut up you jerk. Roger don't pay any attention to him. His so-called humor gets sicker all the time. His brains got scrambled in the rain storm. Come on in. Can I get you anything?"

"Tea would be good," he says as he sits down on the sofa with a slight smile of his face.

"I had to wait until Brown was off duty to do my snooping, so I'm late. That is the bad news. The good news is that I have spotted an employee with a slight limp in the cashier's area and not only do I now know his name, but I have a photograph to go along with the name."

"Roger. You are getting good at detective work. When this is all over, I may have a job for you in my firm which doesn't exist right now."

"When this is all over I may need it. The employee's name is Alfred Cosa. I brought as much data on him as we have in the personnel file."

"After my useless day, I'm so glad to have something to sink my teeth into. I will get right on him first thing tomorrow morning. This is the break we need. Good job, Roger."

"Well. I was only following up on a lead that you produced."

"Ok. It's a team job. It's too bad the third member of the team didn't contribute."

"Be kind, young man. You must know how closely Gineen and I work together at the Casino."

"Don't bother to try and explain anything to him. When you leave, I will try to knock some sense into him with a 2 by 4, Even that might not work on his thick skull."

"Be nice honey, baby."

"Ugh. Sorry for the sick humor."

"Before I go, think about a way to trap this guy in the act. If we are successful in catching him with the goods, I believe he will give us the names of everyone else in the gang, in exchange for a lighter sentence. Don't you agree?"

"My experience tells me that you can never tell how strong a man's resolve is until you test it. In this case, if we catch him with the goods, it will likely be with a relatively small amount. They are pilfering small amounts at a time. My guess is about $10,000."

"That's true and in a local court what you say is probably correct but in a Tribal Court we set our own standards. I can tell you that Mr. Cosa would be facing a very long prison term. It is likely he gives us everything we want to know once we have the goods on him."

"Roger, I like that approach very much and don't doubt that under those conditions we will be successful. Will you able to offer him some sort of witness protection after he serves his term?"

"I hadn't thought about that idea but I'm sure we would be able to offer him a deal if he cooperates fully and is properly repentant during his term, whatever that might be. Perhaps we could even set up a trust fund for him that we would administer and dole out to him over a period of years. We will work something out. I've kept you long enough so unless you have any more questions, I will get on home and leave you to your devices. Good night. Gineen, I'll see you at work tomorrow."

When he is gone, we sit and just stare at each other for a few moments.

"Lover. I not only see the light at the end of the tunnel, but I also see a lovely sight on the other end. The end is really in sight. Isn't it?"

"Yes," I say, "I think so. So, does that make you happy?"

"It does but it is also a little scary. You've been married before and I have not. As the reality sets in I wonder if I will make a good partner for you."

I hold her in my arms and feel a quiver and a little sob.

"Of course, you will. I have no doubts. I will always love you. I guess I just wonder how I will adjust to a new life. Am I just a bad risk? Will I screw up another marriage?"

"You won't. Let's go upstairs and work things out," says Gineen, with a small snicker.

She turns and starts for the stairs and pokes me with her elbow as she does.

"Will you always be a smart aleck asshole?"

"Nice way to talk about your future husband. Hey,

something I was wondering about the last couple of days. Is Roger married? Does he have any family?"

"He was married to a very beautiful woman. She lived with him in the penthouse suite. It's a very sad story which Roger told me a little bit about very recently. They lost a child at birth and his wife never recovered from that. She drank herself to death. I believe that is the reason he has become attached to us and looks at us as the children has never had."

With that we hold each other tightly for the rest of the night.

CHAPTER XII

The very first thing next morning I am on the phone to Sally.

"Sally Langone, how may I help you?"

"Patrick Ingel, good morning."

"Can't talk now, lover. I'll call you back when I can." She hangs up immediately.

"Hey, who were you talking to on the phone?"

"That was Sally Langone, my favorite DMV clerk."

"Oh, that floozy. Did she ask you to come right over and make mad passionate love?"

"Not yet. She couldn't talk to me. Must be office people around her. She said she'd call back later."

"And she called you, why?"

"No. No. I called her."

"What in the world for?"

"Have you forgotten that I have been assigned to look into Mr. Cosa's background?"

"And you can't get anyone else to do this dirty work for you?"

"Well no, I can't as a matter of fact. She's worked well for us for some time and I haven't time to break in someone new, even if I knew who to approach. Which I don't."

"And five will get you ten that the only way she can help you is for you to go to Hartford and meet her for lunch. Another opportunity to try and get you into bed."

"Gineen, certainly you must know by now that there is no way that will happen. Besides, I have made it unequivocally clear to her that it won't happen. She has given up that tack. We are nearly married and it's time for you to develop some trust in me or our married life is going to be very difficult. I hope one day you will meet her. I know that you will like her a lot."

"I know. Still I can be angry at any woman who tries to get you into bed. Can't I?"

"I understand, but we are talking about work here, so please relax. This is wasted energy."

"I will. Thanks for putting up with my nonsense. I'm out the door to work. Give me a hug like you mean it."

As I wrapped my arms tightly around her, I whisper in her ear, "I will always love you no matter what."

"I'm off. You have a good day and I hope you get what you need from Sally."

I hang around waiting for Sally to call back. While I am waiting, I have some thoughts about ways to trap Mr. Cosa with the goods. It would appear the only way will be to watch him every time he leaves the cashier's area. This should be easy since we will know his work schedule. If he really is the culprit and leaves the premises, we must positively know that he is carrying the Casino's cash. Maybe Roger or Gineen can concoct a way for this to happen. Otherwise, if I take him down and he doesn't have the cash, it blows the whole investigation and we might as well go home. Finally, just after ten the phone rings.

"Hello, Arnold Kowalski here."

"And Sally here, *Patrick*! What can I do for you this time as if I didn't know?"

"Alfred Cosa of Norwich. I need to find out everything I can about his past and I need it right away. And don't call me by my real name anymore. It could get both of us in serious trouble."

"Ok Arnold. What does right away mean?

"Means today if you can do it."

"With enough incentive, I could easily get it done today. But I don't want to use a fax or email. Paper trail, y'know."

"Do you think you could get the information by lunch time?"

"Very hard but triple the normal rate makes it possible."

"Jeez, a rip off but you have me in a bind and you know it."

"Don't I, love? Of course, lunch is on you. See you at our favorite restaurant at noon."

"Got it."

I am more than a little steamed at this woman. The money is trivial in the scheme of things, but I just hate to be taken advantage of. I have paid the price in every one of our transactions and she keeps pulling the string ever tighter. I console myself with the knowledge that I will be done with her soon if all goes well. I work off my anger with a quick bike trip to Mt. Misery and a jog to the top. When I get to the summit, there is an attractive woman on my flat rock. More than attractive, beautiful and voluptuous as well. She is wearing short shorts and what looks like a bathing suit top. This place is fast becoming a place to meet gorgeous women.

"Good morning. Great day for exercising out in the fresh air, isn't it?"

"Yes, it certainly is." I tried not to stare at her lovely legs. "Y'know you are on my rock and it's the best one in the neighborhood."

"Really. I didn't see any name plate on it. I am so sorry," she says as she turns to head back down the trail.

"Leaving so soon?"

For the briefest of moments, the old Patrick comes boiling to the surface. I'm not sure if it's her lush body or her Sophia Loren eyes. Or perhaps an inherent character weakness on my part.

"Would you like to join me for a cup of coffee? There is a delightful coffee shop just down the street from the base?"

I quickly come to my senses, "I'm sorry but I have a meeting in Hartford and have to get home and change. Perhaps another time. You take care".

The thought enters my mind that if Gineen and I ever split I might come back here looking for this exotic beauty. I feel a bit guilty letting this thought even enter my mind. At the same time, I know it will never, ever happen. I get on the bike and pedal furiously back home and a shower. The guilt feelings are gone by the time I finish the shower. It takes me an hour to drive to Hartford and another ten minutes to find a parking space. I get a table for two and wait for Sally who is 15 minutes late. She comes in with a copy of the *Hartford Courant* under her arm. She seems nervous as she surveys the place.

"Hello Sally. You are even later than usual. Everything alright?"

"I think so. I am the one taking the risks and it could mean my job and retirement. My situation is risky. I am seriously considering giving it up. Makes me nervous."

"Really. Isn't that a bit paranoid? All cloak and dagger, like a movie?"

"I just won't take any unnecessary chances at this age. We'll see. By the way, when you marry Gineen, let me know. I would like to meet her and watch the ceremony."

"Ok. Did you get the goodies I asked for?"

"Do you really think I would drag you all the way just here to look at your handsome face? Of course I brought it. I gave up hope some time ago that I'd ever lure you into the sack."

"Good. Let's order lunch and see what you have."

"Everything I have is in that newspaper, which you will take when you leave. I prefer that you not open it here. I can tell you the gist of it while we eat. Please order me a small filet with onion rings and a salad."

Eating well is something we have in common. I order the same lunch.

"Now. Make sure that you don't open that paper before you leave town."

"Sally, I already got that message. You sound more paranoid with each passing minute."

She waits for the waiter to bring our meals and then tells me what she knows. "Your Mr. Cosa has a very long history of criminal offenses. He was convicted on some of them and some others, he was brought up on charges and never brought to trial."

"Serious crimes?"

"Well, I suppose it depends on your definition of serious. No murder, homicide or rape. In California, he was sentenced to a 4-year prison term after being convicted of larceny. He served two years and went out on parole for the next two. He disappeared while on parole and California officials would, no doubt, love to talk him, in custody, of course."

"And you are sure you have the right Alfred Cosa?"

"I believe so. The usual driver's license photo is in the package and you can compare it with your man for certainty."

"Anything else?"

"Nope. I didn't trace him any further back than California, but I can if you like."

"No, I don't believe I will need it. I'm sure we have enough."

"Good. Are you and that broad married yet?"

"Not yet but we are close. I expect before too long I will be a married man with kids on the way."

"Does that mean you have knocked her up?"

"Of course not. You have a one-track mind."

"Maybe, but remember, if that woman ever throws you overboard, there are other fish in the sea and I am one of them.

I will probably still be fishing around."

"I'm flattered. But I guess a woman of your beauty and intelligence won't be on the market long if she doesn't want to be. Would you care for some dessert?"

"Nah, just a hug on the way out. And seriously, I wish you and your bride all the luck in the world."

"Thanks Sally." I hug her and slip $1,000 into her handbag.

"Hey Sherlock, that's way more than I asked for."

"I know but you have done your usual great job and it's just a small bonus. I promise when this job is successfully over, I will have a real bonus for you. I couldn't have solved this case without your help. Thanks."

"Not necessary but I won't refuse anything that can add to my retirement fund. You take care."

"Take care, Sally." I may be imagining it, but I think I feel a small quiver in her body and a slight sob. She is out the door in a flash.

I leave the waiter a large tip and walk back to the car that sports a bright red parking ticket. End of a perfect morning. I'll just charge it off to Roger and I feel sure he will pay it with delight after I tell him the news about Mr. Cosa. I keep to the speed limit on the way home. I think to myself, the evidence is piling up with the light at the end of the tunnel getting brighter and brighter. I am nearing the end of the biggest case of my career with a positive ending up ahead. I have several hours before Gineen and Roger show up. I am happy to give up the usual Simonetti House, Templeton house, Mt. Misery hike and all the rest so I stay at the house and watch a movie until they get home. *It Started in Naples,* with Clark Gable and Sophia Loren. The movie is stolen by a cute young kid who couldn't have been more than six or seven. A belly laugh, every time he mouthed a line and he had lots of lines. Gineen will be mad at me for watching it without her, so I won't tell her. I will say I watched *The Godfather* again. She shows up at six with that big hug.

"How did your detecting go today? Did you get what you wanted from the bitch in Hartford?"

"Come on Gineen. I could not have solved this case without her help. You know that."

"I do, but I still feel that she is competition."

"Hey, cut that out. She went far beyond what I asked for."

"Really. How far beyond? Did it include a strip tease, perhaps?"

"Gineen knock it off. For the 300th time there is nothing between us and never will be. She even wished the two of us well in our upcoming married life. I'm thinking we should invite her to the wedding so you two can get to know each other a wee bit. The two of you will get along like sisters."

"Hey, just because we both love the same man it doesn't mean we'd like each other. Oh, never mind. I am acting like the bitch and I apologize. Let's do invite her to the wedding. I'm grumpy and I don't know why. My feelings about her come from fear. Fear that she is better looking than I, fear that she is smarter and more successful than I am. I suppose the ultimate fear is I will lose you to her. It was a long tedious day at the Casino. I kept seeing you in her arms. I apologize."

I grab her and kiss her passionately and whisper in ear, "I love you dearly and I always will. There will never, ever be anyone else. Aside from everything else, I will never lie to you. Oh, and by the way Sally did get us everything we need on Mr. Cosa. His goose is just about cooked because I am sure he is the weakest link in the chain. Once we catch him with the goods, and we will, he'll deliver the rest of the gang to us. Is Roger coming by tonight?"

"He is, but he said he would probably be late so let's go eat now."

"Why don't you go freshen up and I will get some leftovers for dinner?"

When she leaves the room, I gather up some left-over Asian food and set the table complete with candle light and a bottle of champagne I have been saving for a special occasion.

As she walks into the room she exclaims, "Oh what a wonderful sweet man you are and after I've been acting the bitch role, too. Another engagement celebration."

"Well really, the celebration is for the imminent conclusion of the case which will make us rich."

"Oh my."

"Ah, even without the money, I have the greatest asset of all...you."

"I knew there was a reason I love you so much. Better stop all the mush or I will cry again."

"Don't cry now. I hear Roger at the door."

"Hi Roger. Come on in. Have you eaten yet?"

"No, I haven't but don't let me interrupt your dinner. A cup of tea is all I need."

"Nonsense, there is plenty here and more in the fridge. Sit down. I need my adopted father healthy and strong. "

"Well, ok daughter," he says with a small grin.

"You know Roger, it is very unprofessional, but we both have come to love you like a father."

"Stop or you are going to make this old man cry. You'll embarrass me. I see champagne. You kids celebrating something?"

"You got that right. Have a look at this," say I, handing him Cosa's driver's license.

"Looks like a California driver's license for our man Alfred Cosa. You found him. What do we know about his background?"

"Quite a bit. We didn't go back any further than California

and I don't believe we need any more than that. He comes with a criminal background in that state that is serious enough to get him in the tribal jail for some long time. We have him lying on his work application, but we should build a stronger case against him by catching him in the act of making off with the Casino's money. He is the weakest link in their chain. You agree?"

"I do, completely."

"Ok then, let's eat and we'll work on a scheme to catch him on full stomachs."

"I believe I am far hungrier now than I was a few minutes ago. Is there any of that champagne left?"

"Enough for a toast for the three of us." As we raise our glasses, I say, "To the light at the end of the tunnel. May our trip to the end of it be fast and successful."

All three of us down that champagne in one long drink. No sipping here.

"Roger, there is an idea knocking around in my brain. I need some help putting the parts together. We all agree that we need to catch him in the act because it will be a much stronger case against him and thus the threat of a much longer prison sentence. We know when he is subject to stealing cash by just knowing when he is working. The part that I can't figure out is how do we prove the cash he has in his possession came from the Casino?"

"One way to do that would be to mark a code on the bills with invisible ink. Another way would be to use bills with consecutive numbers. We could do both to be doubly sure. We would have to have about $10,000 in bills beforehand and be ready to switch them when he is on the job. The money is not a problem and we could be prepared in advance with it."

"But how do you get it in his hands without tipping him off?"

"I think Gineen or I could do this with little chance of him knowing it. We could divert his attention before he has the cash and make the switch then."

"How do we divert his attention?"

"It would require a well-timed diversion which I think we could do with the three of us working as a team. The movement of the cash out of the cashier's area is timed like clockwork three times each day. You, Patrick, are waiting outside. When the cash is about to leave, Gineen will call your cell. You hang up and call back and ask for Cosa. You tell him his wife has been involved in an accident and could he meet her at the hospital. While he is talking to you I will switch the cash and then ask him to drop it off downstairs at the rear platform where the Armored truck crew will be waiting. When he gets there, you stop him and tell him you are doing a routine security check and then search him. If he's got the cash, we have him cold. If he doesn't have it, we'll try something different the next time. I'm guessing that once a crook always a crook and he will manage to siphon off some of the cash even on the way to the hospital.

"I think we can make this work the first time, which I agree would be the best of all worlds. I will be waiting to wrap my arms around our friend Cosa. Let me know when and I will be ready."

"I'll check the schedules tonight when I get back to the Casino and let you know. In the meantime, get a good night's sleep and if we catch a break it will all end tomorrow. Thanks for dinner, the champagne and most especially the information. Both of you be careful."

"You too, Roger. We will be ready. Good night."

When he leaves, I put my arm around Gineen and guide her up the stairs. "C'mon, lets follow poppa's instructions."

Just as we are about to get into bed the phone rings. It is

Roger. "We are on for tomorrow. All set there?"

"We are indeed. See you in jail!"

A few minutes later Gineen comes out of the bathroom with a concerned look on her face that I notice immediately.

"What's up babe?"

"Probably nothing but I think I felt a small lump in my breast."

"What the hell do you mean, nothing? We'll get you a doctor's appointment first thing in the morning. We can postpone the Casino cleanup for a while. No problem."

"I knew I should have kept my mouth shut. You are a love but like I say it is very tiny and it may not mean anything. Waiting a day or two won't hurt and I am going to the Casino tomorrow morning to help catch Mr. Cosa. I wouldn't miss this for the world."

"But promise me you won't put it off and then forget about it."

"I promise. Cross my breasts...ah, I mean my heart."

"Not very funny."

I toss and turn a good deal that night and don't fall asleep until about 3am. Nightmares all night. We both wake up with a start at seven. Gineen showers first and I follow.

"I'm going to get breakfast at the Casino. Everything goes according to plan, I will see you for a lunch celebration."

"Just, please be careful. I know I've said it before, but we are dealing with guys that will stop at nothing. I need a hug before you go."

I hold her for a couple of minutes and whisper in her ear, "Good luck, wife."

"Nothing is going to happen inside the Casino. You have the hard part bringing Cosa down. You're the one who needs to be careful, husband."

When she has gone, I take out the slip of paper with the

name of the guy we need to get out of the way along with his cell number. Still a bit early but I have no intention of being late, so I drive over to Voluntown and have breakfast in a diner near the Casino. At 9:45, I park outside the Casino and wait for a call. It comes from Gineen five minute later."

"Call the number now." She hung up and I immediately dial the number.

"Hi, this is Carter Alexander. Who's calling please?"

"Mr. Alexander, this is the dispatcher at the Norwich Police Department. I have some bad news for you. Your wife has been in a serious automobile collision."

"Oh no. How is she?"

"Sir. I don't know. All I know is that she has been taken to the Bacchus Hospital. According to my reports from the scene she should be admitted to the hospital at any moment. Is there something we can do to get you there in a hurry? A police escort? We could meet you at the city line."

"No, that's ok. The hospital's so close to the line, it won't be necessary. Thank you for the offer, I'll be on my way in just a few minutes."

"Keep your cell on just in case we need to contact you."

"Thanks."

In the background, I can hear him quickly explain the situation to Roger. Roger tells him to go right away and offers to help him get to the hospital. Alexander thanks Roger for the offer but says he will be ok.

"Then get going. I will take over your duties."

When I hear this, it is a signal for me to move. I get out of the car and walk to the loading platform. I stop and hold my hands up high as I hear an order from the armored car guards.

"Stand still, my friend. We have seen you loitering around here before. What are you doing here?"

I turn around and face them and see one of the guards with

his hands on his holster.

"My name is Patrick Ingel. I'm a private investigator working for the Casino. I can't say anymore because that is my instruction, but if I am correct, you will shortly see an employee come out with some bags of cash for you and some of our money on his person. My job is to take him down and haul him off to the tribal Jail."

"Excuse me, but no one informed us that this was going down."

"I know. It was a last-minute decision. We had no way to anticipate when it would happen."

Just as I was about to suggest he call Roger for confirmation, out comes Cosa looking very casual.

"Good morning fellows. What's with the guns?" He plunks down the big bag of money and starts to head for his car when I approach him. He is toting the little rolling suitcase.

"Just a minute, Mr. Cosa we are under orders to search everyone coming out this door today."

As he begins to react to that order, Gineen comes racing out onto the platform hollering at me, "Patrick!"

With that distraction, Cosa grabs her and puts a gun to her head. I look intently at her and can read her mind. A slight shake of her head and she knees him in the groin.

BAM. I hit him in the right arm causing him to drop the gun.

"Going on a trip, Mr. Cosa? Plenty of clothes in that suitcase or is it full of the Casino's cash?"

"You damn fool the money's back there in the bag. I'm going to sue your ass, whoever you are. Don't you dare touch that suitcase."

"Well, let's see," I say as I open the bag. "Ah, a few nice bundles of cash here in your bag.

"I told you I am going on a vacation and I took it out of my bank this morning. I want to call my lawyer. Let me up you SOB."

I thumb through one of the packets of 100-dollar bills. Sure enough, they are consecutive. I turn to the armored guards.

"Look, there will be substantial rewards to all three of you guards if you keep this quiet for a short while. We know there are others involved in this theft and we don't want to tip them off until we can round them all up. It won't take long, and the Tribal Council is rounding them up as we speak. You can verify the truth of what I am telling you by calling Roger Jones. We may well need you for witnesses."

"No problem, we won't breathe a word."

"You will need a lawyer Mr. Cosa, for sure, but not to sue me or the Casino because we can prove without doubt that this cash came directly out of the Casino Royale. To say nothing of attempting to kill my wife. You, my friend, are headed for a nice long stay in the tribal prison. Pardon me for a moment while I call Roger Jones."

"Hi Roger, this is Patrick and we have him cold with the Casino's money. On top of that, he pulled a gun on Gineen."

Roger arrives and we take Cosa directly to the jail. By this time, he has lost his swagger and remains silent. Roger gets him a cup of coffee and we sit down in a small room that is equipped only with a small table and four chairs. I let Roger take over the questioning because Cosa knows he is the General Manager and he really doesn't know who I am.

"Ok, Alfred. Let me outline your situation. With the serial numbers on these bills, we can prove conclusively that you have stolen thirteen thousand dollars from the Casino today. That's enough to get you confined to this tribal jail for 10 years."

"That's ridiculous. I'll get myself a lawyer. I will talk to the district attorney and make some kind of a deal with him."

"Let me explain something to you. You have been caught in a large theft today. We can probably relate prior losses to shifts when you were on duty. I'm sure we shall find that you have sold no cars in the recent past. I feel certain we will find that your net worth far exceeds what could reasonably be expected from your salary. Furthermore, you are confused. There will be no district attorney, but you can call all the lawyers you can afford but not with the Casino's money. This ground around the Casino is not subject to the control of the of the State of Connecticut. As with all Indian lands it is the Tribal Council that controls and will hear your case. For your further information, I am Chairman of said council. You are in no condition to bargain."

Roger pauses and there is a long period of silence.

"What is it you want from me?"

"That's easy. We want your help in rounding up all the Casino employees who are in any way connected to these past thefts."

"And what's in it for me? They'll kill me if I squeal."

"If you cooperate with us here's what I would recommend to the Council. You will get a minimum jail sentence of 1 year. You will be held here. There will be no possibility that any other members of the gang will ever see you. After that we will do what we can to get you far removed from this area and get you started with enough money to begin a new life. You will be required to sign a pledge that you will never again work in an Indian casino. If you violate that pledge, you will be subject to a full sentence of 20 years. That's it. You must decide right now. Take it or leave it."

There is no indecision on Cosa's part. He is thoroughly defeated. A broken man.

"I'll take your offer," he says in a weak whispered voice."

As soon as he gives us a list of all the Casino employees who are involved in the looting, Roger calls the head of security at the Casino and orders him to pick them all up and take them to the tribal jail. Each isolated in his own cell. We move Cosa upstairs to the jail's administrative office so that there would be no chance anyone would see or talk to him. Within an hour all the members of the gang are in custody, including those who were off duty at the time. A superbly organized operation that would make the FBI proud. Realizing that Roger is in full command of the situation, I pull him aside and whisper in his ear.

"Gineen and I are leaving. I need to take her to the hospital for some tests."

"What in the world for?"

"She has a lump on her breast and insists it is nothing. I am going to get her to the hospital even if I must drag her the whole way there."

"I will say some prayers for her. Please call me as soon as you know the results of the test. Is there anything in the world that I can do? Do you want me to get someone to drive you there?"

"The prayers will do for now. Talk to you later."

I clutch Gineen by the arm and pull her out of the jail to our car.

"Hey. We are missing most of the fun. Where the hell are we going in such a rush? Is there more of this operation going on off the site?"

"No dear sweet lady, there is not. We are taking you to the hospital to get you examined by a doctor."

"No way. I am not going there. I knew I should have kept my mouth shut about that teeny, weeny lump, if it is even a lump at all."

"I don't care how big it is. We are going to the hospital even if I have to use handcuffs to get you there."

I see tears start to form in her eyes and I know right away that they are not caused by my threats. I hug her close and say, "You're scared, aren't you?"

"Yes, I am. My mother died from cancer and I'm afraid it's in my genes. I never told you because I didn't think it was important and I didn't want you to worry."

"Come on, let's go. I promise not to handcuff you."

"Ok". She punches me in the shoulder as we get into the car. At the emergency room of the Bacchus Hospital in Norwich, we wait an hour and a half because we are not an emergency case. The place is busy.

"I knew this was a mistake. Let's go home and I promise to come back when we can get an appointment."

"Not a chance. We'll wait our turn and see what the ER Doc has to say."

While we are waiting, my cell chirps. Roger. I explain we are still waiting a turn in the emergency room. Finally, Gineen's name is called and we go into the examining room to wait a few more minutes for a doctor to show up.

"Good morning, Gineen. It says here on your chart that you have a suspicious lump on your breast. Let's have a look".

She peels off her blouse and bra and he does a little feeling of both breasts. I wonder why he needs to fondle both. It is very uncomfortable to watch, and I want to smack him.

"Is this this the lump you are concerned about?"

"Yes, it is."

"And when did you first notice it?"

"Yesterday."

"Any pain associated with it?"

"No"

"It's good that you came here right away. It's not wise to play games with lumps even if they are very small like this one is. I suggest that you let me make an appointment with a specialist here at the hospital. I'm sure we can squeeze you in tomorrow. I will let the nurse know and she will set you up for tomorrow. You can get dressed now."

We walk in silence to the nurse's station and wait while she arranges an appointment for tomorrow morning. Next stop is the business office to pay our bills with the necessary insurance cards. On the drive to her condo, Gineen puts her head on my shoulder. I don't push any conversation. I know she will talk when she is ready. It is just about lunch time when we get there. Once we get inside, she revives quickly and suggests we go out for lunch.

"But first, take off your clothes and let me make love to you."

"As you say, boss."

"We need to get that glum look off your face."

"Best way I know to do that."

The love is slow and tender. I can't take my eyes off hers the whole time.

"Ok, big guy let's do lunch now. How about sweet and sour cabbage soup at Bubby's Deli?"

"Sounds good to me. I've already had dessert and it seems to have made me hungrier."

Bubby's is a New York style deli that we haven't gotten around to trying yet. Sure enough, they have sweet and sour soup on the menu so that's what we both order with a potato latke on the side. Before the food arrives my cell chirps, and it is Roger. I explain that the ER Doc said it's good we had come in while the lump was so small.

"Roger, Gineen and I are going to get married in the next few days and we'd like you to be there."

"That's great news. I'll not only be there, but if you want, we can have the ceremony in my suite at the Royale and I will arrange everything, including a reception afterwards."

"I'm sure we would both love that, but I will check it with the boss and let you know. What's happening with the gang?"

"The interrogations are going well. We have at least two more members who have verified everything that Cosa told us. We have an iron clad case against all of them. The only thing left is for the Council to decide if we want to try them on the reservation or turn them over to the State."

"Why would you want to do that?"

"Well, there would be certain advantages to that. First, it's a large bunch of people and they would take up a large part of our jail facilities. Then there are the financial considerations. We might want someone else to house and feed them for the next 20 years or so. An expense we don't need. When would you two like the wedding?"

"Tomorrow we are going back to the hospital to see what a specialist says about Gineen's lump, so any day after that would be good."

"Excellent. I will start making the arrangements today and we can do it the day after tomorrow. Is that good for you? I could move it forward to any day you choose."

"The day after tomorrow sounds good. And Roger, thank you so much for doing this. You are a very thoughtful man."

"My pleasure. And by the way, I have deposited a million dollars in your bank account. You might want to find an investment advisor and put the money to work."

I can't speak for a moment. I never expected to make that kind of money for my entire career and now here I am, a millionaire. Well, half a millionaire after taxes.

"Roger. Thank you so much. I guess that was our arrangement, but I had frankly forgotten all about it and had no idea it would be so large."

Lunch is terrific, particularly the dessert, which is cheese cake with strawberries.

On the way out to the car, I get a playful punch in the shoulder.

"In deference to Bubby's lunch, I didn't give you one in the stomach."

"Oh, I am eternally grateful."

"Now we are going to burn off those excess calories. Up Mount Misery. Double time!"

All my exercise runs in the past few weeks have paid off. I keep pace with her all the way to the top, without getting winded.

"Hmm. You're getting good. We'll have to find something more challenging."

"You mean like Kilimanjaro?"

"Hey, we have all that money, we can go there. In style."

"Nice to have a nest egg, woman. Let's not spend it all in one place. Ok then. Mount Washington in New Hampshire, then. Let's do that the day after tomorrow instead of getting married."

"Funny. Home, big guy. Let's relax and spend the rest of the night watching movies. I feel a bit washed out."

"Deal. I get to pick the first dozen titles. No chick flicks."

"In your dreams, but I'll be kind and let you pick the first one."

We spent the rest of the afternoon and evening watching movies and eating snacks.

Next morning it's back to the hospital for our appointment. The oncologist does a thorough examination including x-rays. When he is finished, he sits us down and delivers the news we both anticipated but are not prepared for.

"Ms. Walker, I am sorry to tell you that you have breast cancer. No question about that. That's the bad news. The good news is that you wisely caught it very early. Your chances for a complete recovery are very good."

"What's in store for me?"

"Well, I would recommend radiology treatments at the very least. It won't be easy, and I won't kid you, it will take some time. But you are young and otherwise in good condition, so it will be easier for you than it would be for an older woman."

"I need some time to think about this. Thank you so much."

We leave the hospital quickly and embrace just outside the entrance.

"Oh Patrick, I'm so frightened."

"So am I. But I know you are strong and will come out of this ordeal and be as good as new. I'll be with you all the way and we will search out the best specialist in the country."

"I am so lucky to have you. All I wanted was to marry you and start a family and now this. Please forgive me. I don't want to be a burden to you."

She continues to sob for a few minutes.

"Gineen, in the short time that I have known you, you have brought me more joy than I ever thought I would see. You are not a burden and never will be. How dare you even think that? We are going to get married and we will have a family. It will just take a bit longer. I love you more than life and I would gladly change places with you. Now listen to me. We are going to get married tomorrow and have a good time. Then we are going to search for the best specialist around and I expect that will be in Boston. We will leave this place behind and remember only the good stuff. Do we have a deal?"

"We have a deal."

CHAPTER XIII

At the wedding ceremony in Roger's Suite, we put aside all thoughts of cancer, as best we can, and have a good time. Gineen and Sally meet and immediately warm to each other as I knew they would. As we are leaving, I let Sally know about the cancer.

"Oh no. How terrible, Gineen. Please if there is anything I can do, please, please let me know. You have a good man in Patrick and although I tried my damnedest to seduce him, he never once touched me. You are one lucky dude to have him."

"Yes, I am."

They hug, and both are a little teary. I'm not sure but I think I see a look on Roger's face as he hands Sally a glass of champagne.

After the ceremony and toasts, I take Roger aside and thank him profusely for what he has done for us.

"Roger, Gineen and I are leaving shortly for The Dana Farber/Brigham and Women's Hospital in Boston where she can get the best care."

I give him a hug and so does Gineen. I see some tears forming in his eyes as we leave. A side of this tough old cookie that I haven't seen before. I notice that Roger keeps eyeing Sally which makes me wonder.

At home, we pack clothes and go to sleep after a quick dinner. In the morning, we throw our stuff in the car and take off for Boston.

Made in the USA
Middletown, DE
05 June 2019